A NEW FUTURE

Now penniless and homeless, Flora Lochart felt near despair after her father's funeral. Her sisters-in-law argued over her, hoping for a cheap servant. But it was the marriage proposal from middle-aged Willie Young which panicked her. He saw her as a bargain too. Yet prim Aunt Isa grasped Flora's plight. She gave her a home, love, and protection. At once, a bright new future beckoned.

Books by Barbara Cowan
in the Linford Romance Library:

THE LIVING RIVER
FUTURE PROMISE

BARBARA COWAN

A NEW FUTURE

Complete and Unabridged

LINFORD
Leicester

First published in Great Britain in 1992

First Linford Edition
published 2006

Copyright © 1992 by Barbara Cowan

British Library CIP Data

Cowan, Barbara
    A new future.—Large print ed.—
Linford romance library
    1. Love stories
    2. Large type books
    I. Title
    823.9′2 [F]

    ISBN 1–84617–145–8

Published by
F. A. Thorpe (Publishing)
Anstey, Leicestershire
Set by Words & Graphics Ltd.
Anstey, Leicestershire
Printed and bound in Great Britain by
T. J. International Ltd., Padstow, Cornwall

This book is printed on acid-free paper

Flora Meets Mona

Flora Lochart stood at the sink in the scullery on that dull, depressing day in 1935, her hands in the soapy dish water, watching the busy scene of trams and buses down below in Dumbarton Road.

The street noises were muted from her window, two storeys up in the red sandstone Glasgow tenement. Even in the drizzling February rain she felt a strange envy for the bus and tram passengers and hurrying pedestrians. They all seemed to know exactly where they were going, sure of their destination.

And here she was, at twenty-six years of age, penniless and not even sure where she would sleep tonight. Flora shuddered as the raised voices of her two sisters-in-law came from the big room, arguing over her.

Suddenly, the voice of Aunt Isa

interrupted her thoughts.

'More dishes!' Isa Rennie held up a tray. There wasn't room for two in the little scullery, so Flora began to lift the dirty lunch dishes from the proffered tray and put them in the sink.

'Would you listen to those two!' Aunt Isa sniffed. 'Of course, the one who wins hopes she'll have an unpaid skivvy for life — unless you do something about it.'

'Like what?' Flora sighed, for she knew Aunt Isa meant getting a job. 'Could you get me employment with you in Lambies? Just think of the wonderful experience I have! Preparing the early morning paper runs for the delivery boys at Young's Newsagents — exactly what the best licensed grocers in Glasgow is looking for nowadays!' Flora's voice was heavy with bitterness.

Isa Rennie hated interfering in anyone else's life, but there were things she had to know. 'Have you asked Mr Young if he would take you on full time?' she inquired diffidently. 'It would be so handy, since his shop is just downstairs at the close mouth — and you could afford to keep on this flat, then.' But as her eyes strayed round the kitchen, taking in the worn linoleum, thread-bare sash curtains, battered wooden table and chairs, it didn't seem a happy prospect. Her exasperation at her now-deceased brother-in-law welled up once again. With his tram-driver's pension, they should have been able to live in more comfort than this.

'I did ask Mr Young,' Flora paused. 'And he agreed he could do with my help in the shop all day — and suggested I marry him.'

'He's old enough to be your father! He was in my class at school . . . When did he ask you?'

'Two hours ago — just after the funeral.' Flora sighed.

'Even as a boy Willie Young seldom washed, and he hasn't improved with age.' Aunt Isa shuddered.

Flora turned back to the sink to hide

an unbidden smile. Willie was not quite as bad as that. And he'd meant the proposal in a kindly way. Suddenly, she was aware that there was silence from the next room. Aunt Isa had noticed, too.

'Maybe they've come to a compromise,' Flora murmured.

They both turned as the kitchen door opened. A troubled-looking Robert came in. He was Flora's eldest brother, born twelve years before her, a thin, stooped bank clerk, dark hair receding from his forehead.

'Flora — would you come in now? We think there should be a family conference,' he murmured. 'And we need to get home for the children coming in from school, too.'

The two sisters-in-law were sitting on either side of the fireplace in the high-backed chairs, staring at Willie Young. He sat complacently on the sofa, his elbow leaning on the curved end, a hand supporting his head.

George, her dentist brother, two

years younger than Robert, stood, frowning, with his back to the fireplace. 'Well, Flora, can you tell us what your plans are now?' he asked bluntly.

Flora was puzzled. When she'd left this room to wash the lunch dishes, asking her opinion was the last thing any of them had in mind. Realisation dawned when Willie spoke up.

'I've just told them, Flora, I've made you a good offer. My newsagent's brings me in more than either of them are earning. You don't need their charity. You've a better job with me.' Willie looked round at their faces in satisfaction.

'Thank you, Willie, but . . . but . . . ' she faltered, then took a deep breath and continued haltingly. 'As I said earlier, it's too soon after the funeral to decide anything so — so important.' She stopped, her face pink with embarrassed effort.

'Yes, so she's coming back with me to live,' Aunt Isa put in with a rush. 'And she's going to work with me as my assistant. Rab Lambie's always on to me to get another helper with my coffee and gateaux counter.' Aunt Isa finished, and dug an elbow into Flora for support.

'Yes, yes.' Flora nodded, trying not to show that this was the first time she'd heard Aunt Isa's plan for her future. But a surge of relief ran through her. Willie's proposal had served a purpose. Yet she knew Aunt Isa's offer of a home was genuine. Her kindness would have no strings attached. And to work in Lambies' as well — it was her wildest day-dream come true! Then she saw Robert's wife, Milly, was furious.

Milly stood up. 'I wish you'd told us you had everything all cut and dried. It would have saved a lot of precious time.' She glared at Flora.

'I decided the arrangements after a discussion while we were in the kitchen just now,' Aunt Isa said, being carefully honest.

'I'm glad you'll have some decent prospects with Aunt Isa,' Sally,

George's wife, said kindly. 'If you'd come to me, I'd have let you look after the children twenty-four hours a day, and that's the truth!' she said.

Flora heaved a sigh of relief when her brothers and their wives finally left, five minutes later.

★   ★   ★

There was no money and the furniture was shabby and old fashioned, so a dealer would come to take it away. Her father's books, the only things of worth, would be divided between her brothers.

Flora felt strangely numbed and detached, somehow untouched by the fact that her home for the last twenty-six years was being broken up in an almost casual way. Yet she wouldn't miss having to darn upholstery and hide broken chair springs. She was startled when the voice of Willie Young rumbled behind her. He'd waited in the background and she'd forgotten him.

'Flora, now just give some serious

thought to my proposal. You and me could set up nicely in my place. I would let you furnish it with nice, clean, modern furniture and carpets. And get a painter to decorate it.'

Flora turned and bit her lip as she saw he was hurt and annoyed because she hadn't given the answer he wanted, especially as he thought he was being very magnanimous. Then she noticed Aunt Isa behind him, stiff and bristling with disapproval.

Suddenly, without warning, Flora crumpled. She put her hands over her eyes, and her shoulders shook as tears spilled over.

The other two looked on in amazed discomfort, then Aunt Isa hurried forward, and led Flora back to the big room and set her down on the sofa. She returned to Willie who remained at the door, dumbfounded. Flora was always the most level headed of all his assistants, and never varied in her moods. That was the main reason he'd proposed.

'My niece is overwrought,' Aunt Isa announced in her prim way.

Willie was slow in thinking, but he nodded. 'Maybe I shouldn't have asked her today, but waited a while,' he conceded, sighing deeply. 'But I'm really disappointed. I'd set my heart on getting married.'

'Perhaps your timing was rather unfortunate,' Aunt Isa said in the soothing tone she would use to a difficult customer, as she opened the door wide for him to leave. He shuffled unwillingly out, then they both paused. Someone was bounding up the stairs. After a moment, young Dr Anderson came panting into view.

'You're just the person that's needed, Doctor,' Willie mumbled. 'Flora's in a terrible state — never seen her like that.' He shuffled off downstairs, shaking his head.

Ralph Anderson turned inquiringly to Aunt Isa, who drew him into the flat and closed the door. She spoke in a low voice.

'Perhaps you should know that on top of all her other troubles, Flora has had to cope with an unexpected proposal of marriage from Willie Young.'

'Good grief!' Ralph Anderson exclaimed — Willie Young was an unlikely romantic, everyone took the fifty-year-old for a confirmed bachelor.

'I think it was the last straw when he began to pester her just a few minutes ago — broke down in tears, she did,' Aunt Isa finished.

Flora was sitting on the sofa, red eyed but composed, when they went in. She tried to smile at Ralph Anderson, but didn't quite manage it.

'I'm sorry I didn't manage to get to the funeral,' he said, shaking her hand.

'You've been more than kind,' Flora murmured, feeling tears near again. Ralph had been a good friend, as well as an attentive doctor. She looked away, trying to compose herself once more.

'What are the plans now?' He turned to Aunt Isa for an answer.

'My niece is coming to stay with me and I will have her taken on as my assistant with cakes and confectionery in Lambies' Provision Merchants,' Aunt Isa explained importantly.

'So you'll be resident in Shawlands in the South Side, then,' Dr Anderson remarked to Flora. 'You'll need a doctor locally. I'll give you a few names you can choose from.' He scribbled quickly in a notebook, then tore the page out and handed it to her. 'Next time I'm over Victoria Road way, I'll make a point of coming in and buying sweet things, to find out how you're getting on, Flora.' He smiled, a trace of banter in his voice.

'I hope you do, Ralph — we've been through a lot together.' Flora smiled. 'For a while when Ralph was a medical student he lodged upstairs with old Mrs Linton,' she explained to Aunt Isa.

'And was grateful to do my studying then in this house in front of the kitchen fire. Mr and Mrs Lochart and Flora used to go to bed early, and I would have a couple of hours before the fire died.' He made them laugh with tales of his landlady, whose thriftiness bordered on meanness.

He only left when Flora was completely composed.

★ ★ ★

It was dusk when Flora and her aunt alighted from the tram near Shawlands Cross. The street lights had come on and the light from the shop windows was spilling out cheerfully on the crowded, wet pavements.

Flora shivered — her coat was thin and the rain-laden wind was keen. She knew her aunt was shocked by the contents of her wardrobe, but the pound a week she earned doing the early morning shift in Willie Young's Newsagents had to help support the household. There was no money for luxuries; her father thought buying books and periodicals more important.

When they turned into a close in a

red sandstone tenement, Flora was glad to get out of the wind. But she was impressed by the shining half-tiled walls all the way up to the top landing.

Aunt Isa stopped there, rummaging in her handbag for the keys. The unexpected sound of the door opposite opening made them both turn. A small, stout, grey-haired woman dressed in black came out, closed the door behind her and locked it. The flat had been empty for months, so Isa Rennie was immediately interested in the other woman.

'Excuse me,' she inquired politely, 'can I ask if you're to be my new neighbour?'

The little woman stopped, and stared, unsmiling, at the two in front of her. 'I'll probably be moving in about a week — maybe less.'

'Well, I'll be glad to have someone living opposite again,' Aunt Isa went on, undeterred by the other's cool manner. 'Do you have a family, too?'

'No, there'll be just me — lost my

husband in the Great War.'

'I'm sorry,' Aunt Isa murmured, gesturing slightly to the ring on the third finger of her left hand. 'I lost my fiancé, too.'

'In truth, I'll probably have to get a tenant for the spare room,' the other woman said, unbidden.

'Ah, I see — a paying guest.' Aunt Isa nodded.

At this the other woman smiled wryly. 'Ay, indeed! If things go the way I'm expecting, that's just what I'll have — a paying guest!' She shook her head and gave a deep sigh. 'Well, since we're to be neighbours, I'm Mrs McLaurin. Till today I was the cook and housekeeper in one of the big houses in Pollokshields . . . ' She stopped, as if it was too painful to go on.

Aunt Isa delicately cleared her throat and introduced herself and Flora.

'I'm out on business all day — with Lambies' the Provision Merchants, off Victoria Road,' she explained with some pride.

Mrs McLaurin was impressed at this, and after a few more pleasantries she nodded and thanked Isa. 'Very nice and neighbourly of you to welcome me. Yet it's hard to find yourself unemployed after twenty-five years of service . . . ' She started to descend the stairs with a heavy tread.

★   ★   ★

Later that evening, Mrs McLaurin poked the fire of the four-oven kitchen grate in the large mansion in Pollokshields.

Carefully, she then banked up the fire with small coals. She knew the kitchen door had opened, but she ignored it, concentrating on the task in hand. When she turned and saw the slim girl at the kitchen table her eyes remained cold, until she looked at the girl's chalk-white face.

'You'd better sit down,' she said stiffly. 'It's been a shock for you, too, I see,' she murmured more kindly, when the girl slumped down at the table.

'How — how could my father go off — make all these plans, have everything neatly tied up, and not even give me a hint . . . ?' Mona Alexander whispered through dry lips.

'Ah, well, he did keep saying the business wasn't doing well these last few years, and expenses here have trebled in the same time — but nobody paid any attention. The poor man was at his wits' end.' Mrs McLaurin was briskly matter-of-fact. 'That's why he had to sell up, and tried to see that you, your stepmother, and myself weren't left completely destitute — as Mr Grant, the lawyer, explained.' Mrs McLaurin couldn't hide some bitter satisfaction.

'But I mean, to go off and leave a lawyer to tell us . . . ' Mona shook her head disbelievingly. 'I don't even know where he is.'

Mrs McLaurin nodded. That was what was so much out of character. And it had been an uncomfortable half hour up in the drawing-room, the lawyer telling them in dull, legalistic terms about Mona's father having executed the disposition of the house in his wife's favour — executed a trust in favour of Mona from which she would get three pounds a week, until she married when the residue would be given to her — and also a pension of one pound a week for life for the housekeeper, Mrs McLaurin.

Mr Grant refused to be drawn on where his client had gone, except to say that he had settled all his assets on them.

Now Mrs McLaurin stood and watched helplessly as the girl stood dejectedly in front of her. She was prepared to do battle, speak home truths, but the sight of this heartbroken girl, whom she loved like her own child, wiped all the harsh words away.

'Maybe you'll think seriously of getting married now,' she said kindly.

'No.' Mona shook her head. 'It's all

over. Hamish's mother phoned me just now. She'd just heard about the scandal. Father going off, the business being sold ... She said I shouldn't contact Hamish, that marriage was out of the question. She said I would be just a liability to him in his career ... '

'What?' Mrs McLaurin's eyes blazed. 'Maisie Buchanan should say such a thing! Your dear departed mother, that saintly woman, was real landed gentry. Maisie Buchanan's father was a coalman!'

Mrs McLaurin went on at length about Maisie Buchanan's family. Then she started on the second Mrs Alexander, who had been her husband's secretary, and who had got ideas above her station, too. As far as Mrs McLaurin was concerned, she was to blame for most of the trouble which had come down on the house. And as for Mona, she had given her father much heartbreak by her partying and had hurt those who'd loved her.

Mona looked up at the little woman

and smiled, a little colour coming back into her face. She had heard this tirade often before, and knew perhaps she deserved it. But having all her faults pointed out on a daily basis had made her turn on the housekeeper six months ago, and imperiously remind her of her station as an employee. She knew this had hurt the older woman.

'Yes, Mrs Buchanan is quite right.' Mona sighed. 'It wouldn't be good for Hamish's career just how — a young lawyer just setting out. If the business had been healthy and my father . . . ' She paused, and fought down the emotion speaking of him evoked now. 'Suffice to say,' she continued in a tight, controlled voice, 'I'm going to have to find a place to stay, and probably some way of earning my living — thank goodness for my year at business college!' She gave a dry laugh.

'You'll not find it so easy to walk into a position without experience. There's girls of twenty-one like you who've been secretaries and typists for four and five years,' Mrs McLaurin was quick to point out.

'I know, I know!' Mona cried. 'What else can I do? How can I live on three pounds a week?'

'Three pounds a week! That's a tradesman's wage. Some men are keeping a family on half of that,' Mrs McLaurin said self-righteously, and was about to point out that she had only a pound a week to live on.

But she stopped herself as she saw Mona had buried her head in her hands. 'Look, I've — I've rented a flat in Shawlands. If you like, you could lodge with me.' Her face cleared a little as at once the girl looked up at her with relief, and she went on. 'I need a lodger — I would have to charge two pounds a week, but it would be full board.'

'Oh, that would be wonderful — just the two of us living together!'

Mrs McLaurin made tea, and brought it to the table and the two of them started to make plans for their new life together. The housekeeper was happy that Mona was being so sensible, and that once again she had taken first place in the girl's life.

'When can we move into the flat?' Mona asked.

'I got the keys today,' Mrs McLaurin said, looking away swiftly. 'We can move in when it suits us.'

'Could we sleep there tonight?'

'Tonight!' Mrs McLaurin gasped.

'This isn't my home now — as my stepmother pointed out earlier,' Mona said quietly. 'Nadia ordered me out!' She held up a restraining hand as she saw the housekeeper was again about to explode indignantly. Yet it had wounded her too, for she'd thought she had a good relationship with her father's second wife. So when her stepmother had rounded on her with accusations of knowing of, and even conniving at, her father's disappearance, Mona had been so taken aback that her denials had sounded weak and unconvincing, even to herself.

'Since the place belongs to her, I

won't stay another night under this roof either!' Mrs McLaurin declared disdainfully, and stood up as if ready to do battle. 'I'll get word to Bartie Darroch to bring his van round, and we'll move out tonight. We won't be beholden to that one!'

'Oh, Loly!' Mona stood up and threw her arms round the little woman., 'You're the one constant factor in my life that's unchanged!'

Mrs McLaurin's heart swelled with happiness to hear the girl call her by the childhood name, but she would have died rather than show it.

★ ★ ★

Flora Lochart sat in her aunt's flat in Shawlands, the pretty chintz curtains drawn against the wet February night. She exclaimed as Aunt Isa laid down a daintily-set tea-tray.

'Just a little supper,' Aunt Isa smiled.

Flora had never been in the flat before and was amazed at its feminine comfort. The little scullery held the cooker and sink. A modern, tiled fireplace had replaced the usual cast-iron grate. The floor was covered with a large carpet square, with highly-polished wood surrounds, and the furniture was light and modern, such a contrast to the heavy, dark, Victorian furniture in her old home.

She took the proffered cup, feeling a little overcome. Her aunt had been so kind, insisting she must have at least two weeks' rest before she started working. 'You do think I'm capable?' she asked tentatively.

'Oh, yes, your quiet nature will suit the customers — they don't like brash-ness. But we'll have to do something about your hair and clothes. Someone's coming upstairs!' Isa remarked, and waited as gradually mounting footsteps became audible outside, as if coming to their door. They waited, expecting the bell to ring, and when it didn't Isa rose swiftly and beckoned Flora to follow her.

When they opened the front door,

there was a large young man with bright, sandy-coloured hair setting a travelling trunk down at the opposite door. He turned and his face broke into a huge grin, as he recognised the older woman. 'Hello, Miss Rennie — I didn't know you lived here,' he exclaimed, then nodded towards the trunk. 'Your new neighbours are moving in tonight — quickest flitting I've ever been asked to do.'

'Oh, Flora, this is Mr Darroch, a carrier who brings things to the shop,' Aunt Isa explained, 'and this is my niece, Flora, who's just been bereaved and come to live with me.'

'I'm sorry to hear your father died. Miss Rennie told me about you. And everyone calls me Bartie — it's short for Bartholomew!'

Flora shook his hand, wondered a little that her aunt had discussed her, yet was aware that this young man exuded a comforting kindliness.

'These last weeks, my aunt has been a great support — just don't know how

I'd have managed without her,' Flora murmured.

'Miss Rennie's great!' He nodded enthusiastically. 'She's given me good advice — how to deal with big fancy shops like Lambies' . . . '

He had no time to finish as a young woman, arms full of clothes on coat hangers, rounded the bend of the half-landing beneath them, a pertly-angled sailor hat on her fair curls.

'We're certainly going to live near heaven, up this height!' she joked in a clear, assured voice, as she looked up and saw them standing at the door.

Flora had never met anyone so poised and at ease. She was fascinated by the confident way this young woman held herself as she came up the last few steps towards them, and introduced herself as Mona Alexander.

Mrs McLaurin came puffing up moments later, in a more expansive mood than when they had first met. 'Just decided this evening to move in right away, so we did!' She beamed at them.

'Do you need anything? Milk or tea to tide you over till morning?' Aunt Isa inquired at once.

'I've brought food with me.' Mrs McLaurin indicated the basket on her arm. 'But we might need some kindling to start the fire. I saw this afternoon that there's still come coal in the bunker.'

The two older women started to discuss other provisions that might be necessary, when Mona interrupted furiously. 'Loly! I've just realised — you'd already rented this flat before Mr Grant spoke to us. You knew beforehand about the business being sold and everything!

'Come on, come clean! You know more than you've told me! Do you know where my father is?'

Job Interviews

Flora Lochart and Mona were sitting in Aunt Isa's kitchen. Flora had been surprised to find the dishevelled figure of Mona Alexander at her door that morning, her fair curls blackened with soot, her face smeared with coal dust and her eyes streaming with painful tears. Behind her, smoke had wisped out from the open door.

She had, apparently, attempted to light the fire.

Flora's first instinct had been to help the girl, but she was unsure about becoming involved with her, especially after the stormy scene on the landing the previous evening.

Both she and her aunt had been shaken by the vehemence of the exchange between this girl and their new neighbour, Mrs McLaurin.

However, Flora relented and went

over to the opposite flat to help.

After the chimney had been seen to, Flora invited Mona back to Aunt Isa's for a cup of tea, and the whole story came out . . .

'It came as such a shock.' Mona shook her head. 'Yesterday morning Daddy left as usual — we thought to go to the office. And by early evening there was the solicitor telling us my father didn't intend to come back. It was the start of a waking nightmare!

'Then my boyfriend's mother heard the 'scandal' from some source and phoned to break our friendship. To crown it all, my stepmother, Nadia, ordered me out, for the house and its contents had been left to her. Somehow she's convinced I'm implicated in Daddy's disappearance.' Mona laughed, a little shamefaced. 'I rounded on Loly last night because I thought she knew where my father had gone.'

'And did she?' Flora asked, pouring tea into cups. Mona shook her head. 'No, but she knew he was going to go away. He'd told her and sworn her to secrecy. He got this flat for her and paid the rent for a year, and asked her to offer me a home, if I should need it.'

Mona stopped, perplexed, and rubbed a grubby hand over her forehead. 'Daddy was always so kind and gentle . . . I know he had worries about the business, but that he should go off without telling me, or even Nadia, my stepmother — she'd been his secretary . . . she would have understood. How could he have changed so much?'

'It happens,' Flora said. 'My own father was wonderful — witty, well read, could talk knowledgeably on any subject, although he was only a tram driver to trade. Then my mother died last year, and he just gave up on life.'

'Oh, I'm sorry — rattling on about my troubles when you've just lost your father — at least my father's still alive somewhere,' Mona apologised, and Flora admired the effortless ease with which she switched the conversation to lighter topics.

Soon Flora was laughing as Mona described how she and Mrs McLaurin had coped, sleeping in the flat, with tempers frayed and no furniture. Flora unbent, too, and confided her hopes of working with Aunt Isa in Lambies', and how nervous and afraid she felt about being interviewed.

A little later, Mona stood up. 'Thanks for the tea, and sympathy.' She smiled, putting out her hand and clasping Flora's. 'Maybe you'll influence me to be a better person. You're so calm and kind. Loly is always lecturing me on my faults. She says I'm imperious, impetuous and impractical!' She sighed, then gave a little laugh. 'It's a bit tiresome at times — even if there is some truth in what she says.'

* * *

Mona went back to her own flat, and groaned. It looked so dull and depressing, and the February rain gusting outside the grimy kitchen window added to the chill. A lump of self-pity rose in her throat, but she quelled it fiercely. She was twenty-one. It was time to get on with life on her own. And she jolly well would, she decided, as she stood before the kitchen fire.

This morning Mrs McLaurin had insisted on returning to her post as housekeeper cook, to work out her notice. She refused to pass up any wages due to her.

Mona sat back on her heels, wondering what kind of reception the redoubtable little woman would receive from Nadia, after the curt little note they'd left on the kitchen table saying they were moving out. Her stepmother and Loly disliked each other heartily. Of course, Loly had never accepted Nadia as her mistress. She'd made it very clear since the death of Mona's mother seven years ago that she only took orders from Mona's father, Stuart Alexander. The housekeeper had worshipped her old mistress, because she was 'real gentry.'

As she was washing her hands at the

sink in the little scullery, Mona caught sight of her streaked face in a small, cracked mirror left by the previous tenant. For a moment she stared in disbelief at the grubby face, then her merry laugh pealed round the empty house.

She hurried to put the kettle on the gas ring above the oven on the range. A warm water wash was imperative before that big carrier fellow brought more of their things at lunchtime.

When later Mona opened the door to Bartie Darroch's large smiling person, every curl was in place and there was no sign of soot about her.

'I'm maybe a wee bit late, but I gave Miss Rennie next door a lift home. She's to take her niece to Lambies' for an interview this afternoon,' Bartie informed her as he squeezed into the house with a large trunk. 'Miss Rennie's all worried about what her niece will wear. The poor lassie's hardly got a decent stitch to her back — apparently her father didn't think clothes were important, so Miss Rennie told me.'

As Bartie set the trunk down in the big room he noticed the fire burning in the grate immediately, and Mona felt strangely proud to admit that she had helped in lighting it, with assistance from Flora.

'I'd never have managed on my own. Flora explained to me how chimneys work — this one was cold.' She smiled.

Bartie nodded. 'Couldn't you help her out with something to wear for the interview?' he asked. 'You've got more clothes than a shop!'

Mona was startled at his bluntness. Her first reaction was to rebuff him coolly. But she stopped herself — she'd noticed Miss Rennie treated this tall, sandy-haired young man with defer-ence. And come to that so did Loly, the irascible housekeeper.

'You must have a soft spot for Flora to be so anxious about her welfare,' she said lightly.

'A very fine young woman!' Bartie

Darroch said solemnly. 'I wouldn't mind walking out with her, but she's probably spoken for.'

Mona wanted to giggle. He sounded so old fashioned, but she controlled herself. He was completely serious!

Yet, would it be such a strange thing to do — offer suitable clothes for an unexpected interview, especially to Flora.

Bartie seemed to sense her thoughts. 'It would have to be something in black or grey, since she's in mourning.'

'I've got the very thing!' Mona exclaimed and quickly opened the trunk he had just brought in.

She held up her choice.

'Fine!' He nodded, satisfied. 'Now, I'd best get your beds, chairs and table out of my van, or that wee Mrs McLaurin will be after my blood!'

'Yes, please.' Mona glanced up, laughing. 'I never thought I'd be desperate to see the old furniture from Loly's rooms!'

* * *

Flora Lochart stared at her aunt, appalled that she had to attend an interview so quickly — especially as she could see Aunt Isa was very perturbed about it, too.

'As soon as I told Hugh Lambie this morning that I'd found someone suitable to assist me, he insisted on an immediate interview,' Isa murmured, trying to smooth the wisps of hair which always escaped from their anchoring pins when she got flustered. 'He was quite insistent that it had to be this afternoon. He wants to start you as quickly as possible, if you're suitable.'

'My black dress is clean, and maybe I could wear my mother's pearls to dress it up a bit,' Flora ventured.

'Yes . . . ' Aunt Isa bit her lip. 'But it's really the coat that will be seen. Maybe I'll have something that you could wear.' She frowned, and hurried through to her wardrobe. She knew already there was nothing suitable for a young woman of Flora's age.

The door bell jangled and Aunt Isa

closed her eyes distractedly.

'Surely that's not Mr Darroch here already to take us back to the shop,' she exclaimed. But when she opened the door it was Mona Alexander who stood there with garments over her arm.

'Just heard about Flora's interview. She was saying this morning that she hadn't got anything suitable to wear, so I wondered if she'd like to borrow these.' She held up a three-quarter-length coat in flecked black and grey fine tweed, with a matching skirt, a black blouse with a large bow at the neck, and a small black hat with a veil.

Isa Rennie saw their excellent cut and knew how much they would enhance Flora's appearance at the interview. Normally she would have politely refused the offer, but this was no time to stand on dignity. Yet, even so, she hesitated. It was difficult to accept.

'Flora helped me this morning — indeed, she saved my sanity and gave me tea — so it would salve my conscience a little if she would accept some help from me,' Mona wheedled. 'It should be the right length for Flora — I got the outfit a couple of years ago, when the skirts were very long.'

'Since you put it that way,' Isa said, mollified, 'I'll persuade Flora to accept your offer. Do come in!'

When Bartie Darroch returned to give them a lift back to the store he stared hard at Flora, now a little self-consciously wearing the attractive outfit. She was still very nervous and excited, never having attended an interview before. Aunt Isa had assured her it was a foregone conclusion that she would be employed, but Flora was afraid to count on it.

Getting a position with Lambies' would be like a daydream come true. She'd often walked from Partick to the Byres Road branch for some of their specially-cured bacon as a tea-time treat, and dreamed of working there.

Bartie's smile was openly admiring. 'Hugh Lambie's lucky to get such a fine woman as an assistant,' he said gallantly.

Flora gave him a nervous smile.

'Do they need another assistant, or typist, bookkeeper, or whatever? I'll try anything!' Mona put in, laughing.

'Oh, no, there wouldn't be anything to suit you,' Aunt Isa said gently, unwilling to be hurtful, but such a volatile personality as Mona's would not be suitable for Lambies'.

'Yes, there is!' Bartie Darroch cried. 'Mr Hughie was saying that he needed an accounts clerkess.'

'No! No!' Aunt Isa was scandalised. 'That wouldn't be a position for such a young . . . refined person as Miss Alexander.' She always tried to ignore the fact that Lambies' accounts clerks needed special diplomatic skills and a certain steeliness of character. She cleared her throat delicately. 'It's not just keeping accounts that's involved, but also pursuing arrears!' she explained in a pained whisper.

'I could do that. This last few weeks

I've even had some experience of being on the receiving end — although at the time I thought it was all a mistake,' Mona admitted.

'Get your coat on, and come with us. I'll tell Mr Hugh I brought you for the job,' Bartie announced, and made for the door. 'We'll give you five minutes — we'll be waiting in the van.'

With a whoop of delight, Mona dashed back to the flat, and reappeared in minutes wearing a belted fawn trenchcoat and brown hat on her fair hair.

Flora remembered little of the journey, except that the four of them were crammed into the cab of Bartie's van. Yet, at their destination, even in her highly-nervous state, she noticed at once that the Crosshill branch of Lambies' High Class Provision Merchants had the same kind of mahogany magnificence as the Byres Road branch, with which she was more familiar.

The great counter ran in the same horseshoe fashion, the wood gleaming, the counters inset with marble on top, the shining brass scales ranged round at the same precise intervals, although the more modern white spring scales were in evidence, too. Even the smell was the same — a strange mixture of ground coffee, bacon, cooked meats and whisky. The only difference was the kiosk in the middle of the shop, piled high with fancy cakes, chocolates, and many other mouth-watering concoctions.

Aunt Isa introduced Flora to Mr Hugh Lambie, one of the two brothers who owned the business. Then she had to leave immediately, to take up her station within her specialised stand.

Mr Hugh was a bluff, grey-haired figure in a white coat overall. And after only a few questions, standing in the middle of the shop, he shook her hand.

'Yes, you'll do!' he boomed. 'I knew when Isa finally found a girl to help her, she would be exactly right. Start tomorrow morning at eight.' He turned on his heel beckoning to Mona who was waiting near the door.

Flora stood uncertainly. Was that all? The interview hadn't even taken two minutes.

'Wait for me!' Mona hissed as she passed, then followed Mr Lambie out of sight into the back shop.

'He'll have to give her a full interview, since he doesn't know what she's capable of,' Aunt Isa murmured, her hands busily arranging her stand. 'Perhaps Mr Darroch is right — such a forthright young woman might be just the person to cope with the unpleasantness of following up arrears. Ask her to tea this evening and we'll hear how she got on.'

Then Isa craned her neck, peering over at the rolls of hams and bacons behind the opposite counter near the gleaming hand slicing-machine. She pointed. 'Get half a pound of Belfast ham from that third ham from the left. We'll have ham and eggs, and these French cakes for after.' Aunt Isa handed a neatly-packaged box over to Flora.

There were few customers about and Flora felt a little shy of going over to the counter where the three young male assistants watched her with unabashed interest. But when she approached, they turned away, all suddenly busily occupied. She stood for some moments waiting before a loud reproachful cough came from Aunt Isa. Then one of them came to serve Flora with an exaggerated politeness that bordered on insolence. She was suddenly aware of antagonistic undercurrents which these three took no pains to hide from her.

It was a relief twenty minutes later when Mona bounced towards her, eyes shining. She had got the position. 'I'm starting tomorrow,' she whispered loudly to them. 'Come on, Flora, let's celebrate — afternoon tea's on me!' And she linked arms with Flora as they left the shop.

To Flora, who'd seldom left Partick, her home district, going up town was always an occasion. But she could see that for Mona it was an everyday occurrence, as she confidently led the way on and off trams, and into a very fine teashop in Buchanan Street. Normally she would have been over-awed by the opulent surroundings, but Mona treated it all in such a matter-of-fact fashion, ordering afternoon tea with practised ease from the waitress in a frilled cap and apron, that Flora relaxed.

Mona was in high spirits, vastly pleased that she had found a position, despite Mrs McLaurin's forebodings about her lack of office experience.

'It's almost a year since I did the business course, so I was worried my skills might be rusty. But their books are very simple, although I almost died when Mr Lambie gave me a letter.' Mona giggled. 'When I came to type it I couldn't read all of my shorthand, so I took a chance and typed the letter more or less in my own words. And guess what? He congratulated me on putting his words into better English! I couldn't — '

'Hello, Mona!' A tall young man in a dark business suit and black overcoat, carrying a bowler hat, stopped at their table. He looked pleased to see her.

The happy smile on Mona's face changed to a defiant mask. 'Hello, Hamish! And how is Mummy's boy?'

'Why didn't you tell me things were bad with your father?' he asked, ignoring her jibe. 'I might have been able to help.'

'It's a very long story, which everyone is prejudging. But tomorrow I become a businesswoman, so I won't be seeing any of the old crowd again — including you,' Mona said, trying to sound flippant.

Flora sat feeling uncomfortable, for she knew from what Mona had said earlier that she was very fond of this young man. When his mother had phoned to break off their relationship, it had hurt Mona very deeply. Flora could see why. Hamish was very handsome

44

and his direct way of talking was pleasingly attractive. She found herself blushing as his gaze focused on her, and she suddenly wondered with a pang if he recognised that she was wearing Mona's things.

After a few minutes of trying to speak seriously to Mona, he stiffly bade them goodbye and walked out angrily.

'Well, that's the end of that!' Mona sighed, pushing her cream cake round her plate with a fork. 'The thing is, I agree with his mother that I wouldn't be good for him now he's setting out on his career.'

The unexpected meeting had drained all the gaiety from Mona, and she gratefully accepted Flora's invitation to come to tea.

'Oh, thank goodness,' she said. 'Loly won't be home till about eight o'clock and I don't fancy my own company very much right now. There are too many unanswered questions swirling around in my mind. Not least that I should have given Hamish the chance to explain.'

Back at her aunt's flat in Shawlands, Flora poked the fire into life, and pulled the chintz curtains to blot out the foggy dusk, while Mona curled up quietly in an armchair.

Flora sensed the younger girl was in a sad mood after meeting her young man this afternoon.

Yet, she envied Mona knowing someone so vibrant and attractive. The only suitor she had had in her twenty-six years was the fifty-year-old, paunchy, balding newsagent, Willie Young. And when he'd proposed after the funeral, she was sure it was because he saw her mostly as a useful, unpaid assistant.

Flora was no use at small talk, so stayed silent as she prepared the meal, leaving Mona to her own thoughts. But both of them perked up when the front door opened and Aunt Isa's clipped tones, mingling with a deeper male voice, came through to them in the living-room.

'Set another place for tea, Flora,

dear. I've brought Dr Anderson — he has a book he wants to return to you,' Aunt Isa said happily.

'I was at the Victoria Infirmary, and I dropped into the shop to see you'd moved safely.' Ralph Anderson shook Flora's hand.

★ ★ ★

Mona became alert when she realised that the visitor was a doctor. During the meal she explained her father's actions to him, and plied him with questions about stress and anxiety symptoms, and whether they could make a person act out of character.

Aunt Isa had not heard Mona's history before, and she listened, round-eyed and engrossed. Such goings-on were outwith her usual experience. And it greatly surprised her that this rather bold girl was so very well connected.

Ralph patiently answered the questions and tried to reassure Mona.

It was only as he was leaving that he

referred to his real reason for seeking Flora out — a small book of Burns' poetry which her father had loaned him some time ago.

Flora took the book gladly, her fingers smoothing the covers for it was like an old friend.

'I bought my father this book when he retired. It cost me seventeen and sixpence.' She smiled, opening it up and pointing to the flyleaf and the inscription she had written at the time.

'It's a pity you wrote on it, for that might cut down its value,' Ralph said regretfully. 'You do know it is a very early edition of Burns's poems?'

Flora felt a pang of disappointment. She'd never thought of the money value of the little book, only the pleasure it gave her father when she presented it to him. She had put in extra hours of work after school in Mr Levison's second-hand book shop to painstakingly pay for it a florin or halfcrown at a time. Mr Levison cut the price for her because the book would be treasured. And that was important to the old book dealer.

'Where are the rest of your father's books?' Ralph asked.

Flora explained that her brothers had taken them between them. She'd known she dared not bring them here as Aunt Isa disapproved of all the books her father owned. His pursuit of knowledge was an expensive luxury which Aunt Isa thought scandalous.

'I hope they realise that some of them are probably unique.' Ralph remarked.

'You'd better mention it to Milly, Robert's wife. She's the type who would think if a book was old that it was only fit for the midden,' Aunt Isa said a little waspishly.

'That did come into my mind,' Ralph said ruefully, for he had heard about the humourless Milly and her houseproud ways.

Somehow Flora was glad when Ralph went away. For someone who was gently caring with physical ailments, he seemed amazingly insensitive to her feelings.

It was upsetting to discuss her father's books in terms of value so soon after his death — especially as she had shared his interest in them, reading and re-reading them, too.

Mona was more cheerful after her talk with Ralph. It had helped her understand, and perhaps forgive a little, her father's actions. And for the first time she wondered how he was managing to live, since all his assets were settled on herself, Nadia and Loly.

But Ralph thought since he had planned his disappearance in such detail, that he would have planned his survival, too.

Nobody's Fool

Mona Alexander waited with Flora and her aunt until footsteps were heard coming upstairs.

'That will be Mrs McLaurin now, I think!' Aunt Isa said, looking at the clock on the tiled mantlepiece which was showing eight-thirty.

'Oh, yes.' Mona giggled. 'Just wait till I tell her that I've got a job.' And she hurried towards the front door. She opened it, but quickly closed it again in alarm. 'Oh no! She's got Nadia, my stepmother, with her — and Hamish!' She stood with her back to the front door, and looked at Flora and Aunt Isa beseechingly. 'I can't . . . I can't . . . not all three of them!' she whispered, her lip trembling and tears coursing down her face. Suddenly, she had no energy left to do battle.

Flora was dismayed. Was this weeping, vulnerable figure the wordly-wise girl of this afternoon? Yet she could sympathise, remembering her own breakdown after her father's funeral when everything got too much.

Isa Rennie understood the situation at once, and took command.

'Flora, take Mona into your bedroom until she feels a little more composed. I will have the three of them in for some tea — and Mona, come through when you feel you can face them,' she said firmly. 'I'll tell them you're having a lie down.'

Flora went forward and put an arm round Mona's shoulder and with no demur led her towards the bedroom.

'Have a good cry, dear. You'll feel a lot better.' Aunt Isa patted the girl's shoulder as she went past, and pressed a clean handkerchief into her hand.

'You're so very kind!' Mona tried to stem her tears with the handkerchief.

In the bedroom, Flora sat quietly beside Mona on the edge of the bed, and waited for the weeping to stop, and not long after admired Mona's entrance into the living-room, head held high, her voice light. Except for her tear-reddened eyes she seemed not to have a care in the world.

'How nice of you to come and visit, Nadia,' she said, nodding to the tall, well-dressed woman sitting in the fireside chair. And she gave an airy wave to Hamish in his business suit and heavy dark overcoat over by the window.

Mona's stepmother was beautifully dressed, her make-up faultless, but Flora sensed that despite all this there was strain on her face, and an air of exhaustion about her.

'Mona, please come home. If . . . I mean *when* . . . your father comes home, I want him to find the family complete and waiting,' Nadia said in a strained voice, glancing apprehensively at the little housekeeper, who sat with a self-righteous expression on her face.

'I won't interfere!' Mrs McLaurin

sniffed. 'Mona is free to do just exactly what she wants.'

'I appreciate your offer, Nadia.' Mona went forward and kissed the seated woman. 'But I've decided to stay with Loly because I've got a job — I start tomorrow and I've given this address.'

'See, I told you you were just wasting your time! Mona asked to come to live with me.' Mrs McLaurin was triumphant and drained her cup with a flourish.

'More tea, I think, Flora.' Aunt Isa made signs to her niece.

Flora lifted the teapot and started to refill the cups while Mona cheerfully described her interview this afternoon.

As she was refilling Hamish's cup he spoke in a quiet, urgent voice. 'Is this a proper sort of position Mona has got herself?'

'Oh, yes, in fact we both start tomorrow at Lambies' in Crosshill,' Flora assured him. 'They are a top-class firm. My Aunt Isa works there.'

'Lambies'. Oh, good — that's a relief. I came tonight to check that it was a proper position. Mona can be so impetuous,' Hamish said, looking up at this tall, slim girl with the calm air he'd noticed this afternoon. 'I'm glad she'll have you near. I think she needs a friend.'

★ ★ ★

But over the next weeks it was Flora who was grateful to have Mona as a friend. Working with Aunt Isa was not the pleasant experience she had expected.

Her aunt had tended her counter for a long time single-handed, and had her own particular ways of doing things.

Flora was very nervous, but found it irritating to have her aunt constantly rearranging things she had done. And for a week she was not allowed to serve customers, but only tie up their purchases.

It only took her days to understand

the coolness between the three young men on the ham counter and her aunt. Aunt Isa watched their every move, and felt it her duty to report to Hugh Lambie if she thought their conduct was not suitable for Lambies'.

Yet, it was they who'd alerted Hugh Lambie when they saw Willie Young at the cake counter upsetting Flora with his remarks. And after that Tom, Dick and Harry, as they were nicknamed, befriended Flora, and brightened her day by their antics — behind Aunt Isa's back!

'Don't worry, we'll watch out and see that old man doesn't pester you again. We're sorry for you being under the Dragon's thumb all day,' Tom Miller murmured to her at the end of her first week. 'She'll not let you breathe on her customers.'

It was Hugh Lambie himself who intervened. 'Isa, I'm not paying a full wage to your assistant for you to have her wrapping. I could get you a fourteen-year-old for that. Let her at least serve the passing trade,' he said, adding. 'And she can take over on her own while you're having your lunch, and a proper tea-break. That's why you'd to get help.'

* * *

One lunchtime three weeks after starting in Lambies', Flora was on her own at the cake counter when Nadia Alexander came in. She and Mrs McLaurin had taken to shopping here since Mona got the position in the office. For a moment Flora didn't recognise her, she looked so ill.

Nadia stood at the counter, swaying a little.

'Mrs Alexander, are you all right? Please — won't you sit down?' Flora gestured to a chair which stood by the counter.

Nadia nodded and eased herself on to the seat. 'I've people coming for bridge this afternoon. I need some cakes and savouries.' She sighed heavily.

Flora quickly filled the special fancy cardboard boxes with the order, her eyes darting to watch the woman sitting on the other side of the counter.

Then Nadia looked up and saw the concern on Flora's face, and tried to smile. 'I don't know what's wrong with me. Anyone I speak to, even the doctor, tells me it's my age,' she murmured. 'I've always been healthy so I'm not taking this very well. You wouldn't know a sympathetic doctor, who would listen to me giving a bizarre set of symptoms and not think I'm just a silly forty-year-old woman?'

Flora thought of Ralph Anderson. He had been so gentle, listening to and answering Mona's questions about her father's behaviour, and he'd been so attentive to her parents in their illnesses.

'Yes, I do know a doctor who would treat you seriously. Here's his address and telephone number.' She scribbled them on a price pad and passed it over.

'Thank you — thank you very much.

You are the only one who has inquired,' Nadia said, her eyes suddenly filled with tears. 'I really don't feel right — haven't for months. I'm exhausted!'

After Nadia had gone Flora wondered if she had done the right thing. She was sure Aunt Isa would not approve. But her mother, if she were alive, would have said that Nadia was a 'bad colour.'

She looked up at the office windows above the licensed counter at the end of the shop and saw Mona looking down, making faces at her. She had obviously seen her stepmother come in.

As it was Friday and the shop remained open till seven-thirty in the evening, Flora met Mona in the back shop late in the afternoon, where they were allowed to have a twenty minute break to have a snack. On the other weekdays the shop usually closed at six o'clock.

Mona was eager to know why her stepmother had called, and was surprised that she should buy savouries and cakes. 'Nadia always took such a pride in preparing her bridge party things,' she puzzled, then smiled. 'Loly always got mad at her being in the kitchen, especially as Nadia has a real flair for making fancies and presenting them well, while Loly is merely a competent home baker and plain cook.'

'I think she was a bit under the weather,' Flora said seriously.

'Probably missing my father. She's crazy for him — always was,' Mona murmured, off-hand. Her face brightened as Bartie Darroch came in, a side of ham over his shoulder. She held up the teapot and called to him.

'There's a cup of tea here.'

He grinned widely when he saw them and signalled that he would soon be there. He brought in more hams and then came across.

'Don't usually work so late on pay-day.' He smiled, taking a chair beside them. 'But when you're building up a business it's bad policy to pass up jobs — and this one was a special for

Mr Hugh.' He jerked his head over to the heavy wooden, butcher's-type table where Mr Hugh and Tom Miller were already busy boning and rolling the hams.

'Do you work for yourself — you're not an employee?' Mona asked.

'I'm my own master!' Bartie exclaimed with satisfaction. 'Mind you, the family have always been carriers, and coal merchants. The Darroch carts you see about the place — they belong to my father. I reckon the future is in motors — vans — but my father disagrees, so I got my own van and set out to prove him wrong.'

'And have you?' Flora asked.

'No!' Bartie grinned. 'Now I reckon that there's still room for the horse and cart — and the van. But the van will win in the end. And I'm going to have a fleet of them.'

'Did you quarrel with your father over it?' Mona asked almost eagerly.

'No! No!' Bertie shook his head

good-naturedly. 'He's complacently sitting back waiting for me to fail, since I'd no proper experience of the actual work involved being a carrier — I'd only worked in the office taking orders.' He went on to describe his difficulties setting up on his own — trying to get loads, doing small removals, and finally, through Aunt Isa's recommendation, carrying for Lambies'.

'I'm beginning to make a nice wage, now,' he said with satisfaction.

'Good! You should be able to take two nice young ladies like us out for supper, then,' Mona suggested brightly.

'Now I would like that very much.' Bartie delightedly smacked his hand against the table. 'And what evening would suit you, ladies?'

'Tonight!' Mona replied pertly.

'Oh, dear, not tonight — I've got a wee removal to do. And I couldn't let the folk down.' Bartie's face fell, but then he brightened. 'Maybe next Friday, at one of the big restaurants in town — I could book a table for the three of us.'

'Marvellous!' Mona cried.

Flora was aghast at Mona's forwardness, yet helpless as to what she could do about it. The whole thing had been conducted in such a light-hearted manner, that to object would seem surly. But when Bartie left them she rounded on Mona.

'You shouldn't have done that!'

'Yes, a very improper thing to do,' Mona said gleefully. 'But I like Bartie — he's so open and direct. There's nothing devious about him. Anyway, we could both do with a night out.'

'But I'm still in mourning. It's not six weeks since my father died!' Flora said.

'It's not a place of entertainment — it's just a meal.' Mona demolished her objections.

Flora was unsure, and yet she did want to do something a little different. She was very fond of her aunt, but her company both during working hours and at home without a break was tedious.

'You can come over to my place tonight and we'll get something in a suitable colour for you to wear out of my trunk,' Mona finished in a very determined tone that brooked no more argument.

At seven-thirty the doors of the shop were closed and the staff relaxed.

'Must say, I appreciated your help today,' Aunt Isa told her niece. 'Best day for sales ever. You've really got the feel of the cake and confectionery counter now. Even the customers have accepted you.'

These words of praise from her aunt lifted all fatigue from Flora's shoulders. And that evening for the first time she left the shop with a sense of satisfaction.

* * *

Mona joined them as they took the tram to Shawlands. 'I'll have to get my own tea tonight,' she grumbled. 'Loly has gone back to see Nadia. She seems quite worried about her. Loly has worked her notice by now — but she still goes up every day on some pretext or another.' Mona disliked having to look after herself, especially when it involved cooking.

'We're having Irish stew tonight.' Aunt Isa smiled. 'You're welcome to share it with us.'

'I love Irish stew!' Mona brightened. She liked eating with her neighbours. Somehow, Aunt Isa, with her attention to detail, reminded her of her mother presiding at meals when she was young. And the flat was so neat and comfortable, the decoration fresh and inviting.

And Isa Rennie had a special soft spot for the younger girl. Secretly she admired Mona's high spirits, and how, despite them, she had settled to work at Lambies'.

She'd impressed Hugh Lambie by the way she tackled the work, especially her success in dealing with customers who were slow to pay their accounts. She was able to speak about this sensitive subject with ease, and no umbrage was taken. Hugh Lambie thought she had a rare gift.

⋆　⋆　⋆

That Friday had been a fine sunny March day, but now the evening air was crisp and cold, so Mona was glad to reach Isa Rennie's top flat in Shawlands. She loved Isa's living-room and still marvelled at how quickly the fire caught and the room became warm and cosy.

She also admired the way Isa and Flora always got up in plenty of time each morning to clean out the fire and reset it ready for their return in the evening, tidying the flat, too, so that it was welcoming. Somehow she could never get up in time to do all these things. It took all her energies to have a little breakfast and then look out clothes to wear.

Mrs McLaurin, although she was the housekeeper in her old home, was used to having daily helps to do the heavy work, and was reluctant to do housework. And Mona didn't know how.

After their supper, Aunt Isa indulgently sent the two young women to choose something for Flora to wear when Bartie took them out for supper next week. She enjoyed the new dimension the two young women had brought into her life these past few weeks. Although she had never married, her fiancé having been killed in the Great War, she was a romantic. And she'd noticed how Bartie admired Flora. They would make a nice couple — Flora with her quiet dignity, and Bartie so kind and hard working. Not that she would interfere or even hint, of course.

When Flora went across the landing into the flat opposite, she understood why Mona was always so pleased to be invited to Aunt Isa's.

The woodwork here was dark brown,

as were the doors, and flimsy curtains fluttered at the windows from constant draughts coming through the loose frames. The furniture was sparse and badly placed, and the cold fireplaces spilled over with ash and cinders.

There were several large travelling trunks standing in the big room which served as Mona's bedroom. Mona went to the only one which was locked and opened it up.

'See, there's plenty of black, grey and navy in here. Take your pick,' Mona said gesturing grandly. Then, as she saw Flora was embarrassed about rummaging through her clothes, she took a quick look and brought out a black crepe dress and bolero, with a pleated white organdie jabot at the neck and the same white organdie pleats on the cuffs and the bolero.

'You'll be able to carry this off,' she announced, thrusting them at Flora, who took them reluctantly.

'These haven't been worn!'

'No, very little of what I have in that

trunk has. Changed my mind about them after I bought them.' Mona tugged the labels off. 'Put them on, and then we'll try some of the others.'

Flora tried on the dress and bolero and, like the outfit for the interview, which she had since bought from Mona for 12/6d, this outfit looked as if it had been tailored for her.

'Yes — oh, yes!' Mona cried delightedly. 'You look like a princess in that! I looked like a child dressed in adults' clothes.'

They spent almost an hour looking through the trunks and trying on outfits. But in the end the first outfit was chosen and Mona agreed to sell it for 10/-.

Flora was amazed that Mona had so many clothes which she had not worn. Everything she herself owned had been sponged and pressed countless times. And from what Mona said there were almost as many clothes again still at her old home. Perhaps there was something in Mrs McLaurin's claim that the business had failed through Mona and her stepmother's extravagance . . .

'Keep it on — let's go and show your aunt!' Mona exclaimed.

They trooped back to the other flat, Mona flinging open the living-room door, announcing, 'Princess Flora of Partick!'

Laughing at the absurdity of it, Flora went in. Suddenly she realised her sister-in-law, Milly, was sitting in one of the fireside chairs.

Milly's eyebrows arched in surprise when they entered. 'You seem to be recovering well from your bereavement, Flora,' she murmured, her eyes taking in every detail of the attractive dress and bolero.

Flora introduced Mona to her sister-in-law as another employee of Lambies', but she saw Milly's narrowed eyes noting the expensive shoes and clothes that Mona was wearing. They were not the usual cut for an office girl, and Milly fixed everyone's worth by their clothes.

★ ★ ★

It was some time later, as they were taking tea and biscuits, that Milly got round to her real reason for visiting.

'I met that nice young Dr Anderson,' she started, 'and he was remarking on what a fine collection of books your father left. As a matter of fact, he was quite lyrical about them.' She smiled sweetly. 'Indeed, he said we should have them valued.'

Flora was horrified to hear that her brother, Robert, had spoken to one of his bank's clients who was an authority on books.

'We were quite amazed to discover we could get £1000 for the collection,' Milly finished in triumph.

'Oh, no, you aren't thinking of selling them!' Flora gasped. They were so much part of her father that it seemed unthinkable.

'Not me! I have no say in the matter,' Milly rushed to clear herself. 'But Robert and George have been discussing it. As married men they could use the money — several hundred pounds could buy a nice bungalow, or a car,' she finished almost accusingly.

'Yes, I suppose so.' Flora sighed.

'There is just one thing — I believe you have in your possession a valuable edition of Burns' poetry. That should really go in with the rest.'

At this Isa Rennie saw her niece recoil as if she had been struck. Aunt Isa's temper rose for the knew that book Dr Anderson had brought back to Flora meant a great deal to her.

'Flora gave that book as a gift to her father when he retired — bought with her own money. Selling it is the last thing she has in mind. After all, it's the only thing she has to remind her of her old home,' Aunt Isa said in a tight little voice. 'You'll remember she was told a dealer was taking everything — although there were a few ornaments besides the books that didn't go to the dealers — I made it my business to find out!'

Milly jumped to her feet, her face scarlet. 'They're worth nothing. I — we — Sally and I — thought our husbands would like to have ornaments from their old home about the place.'

'Maybe so — but I wouldn't have minded certain ones either, for they belonged to my mother,' Aunt Isa informed Milly very politely.

Flora listened in some bewilderment. It was the first time she had heard of the ornaments. After her father's death she had been so tired that she had not really given this business end of his affairs much thought. She'd left that to her brothers.

'You've really got it all worked out between you!' Milly blustered.

'Oh, no, my dear! There's not been one word between Flora and myself about her father's affairs. She knows very well I disapproved of him spending their money on books when it should have gone to making my sister's life more comfortable. Indeed, I haven't even asked her if she got her share of what little the dealer paid for the furniture,' Aunt Isa added.

Milly glared at the prim, bespectacled figure. 'I'll see Robert, and she'll get whatever is her due.' Her voice was shrill as she realised the visit had gone awry. She'd thought her husband's aunt was a timid, genteel person, and it would be easy to come here and collect the missing book from Flora, who was always subservient.

But while Isa Rennie might act lady-like, underneath she was nobody's fool. And this Flora, dressed like a mannequin, was changed out of all recognition from the crushed, apathetic person at the funeral. And worse still, that Mona Alexander person was sitting looking on, as if she was amused — perhaps even laughing at her.

In the last five minutes Milly's self-esteem had been unexpectedly battered. She was at a loss and a little frightened, so she began to bluster.

'Mind you — we'll consult a lawyer about that book. It should be with the rest.'

'Oh, no!' Flora gasped, sick at heart. She didn't want her father's books fought over. He'd never thought possessions were important. 'I'll give you the book,' she said quietly and got up.

'Indeed you will not!' Aunt Isa stood up to bar her way. 'Let them get a lawyer in and have things settled according to Scots law. Then you'll get your fair share of whatever is going, instead of being overlooked as the unmarried daughter who has no standing in the eyes of her sister-in-law when there's a share-out.'

Milly stood for a moment glaring angrily at Isa, almost ready to confront her, but thought better of it.

'Don't trouble to see me out — I'll manage!' she said coldly, trying to regain her shredded dignity. And she marched out.

'Gosh! That was exciting,' Mona breathed. 'Although I honestly believe she hadn't even counted Flora as a beneficiary.'

Aunt Isa turned and nodded, a little smile on her face. 'If I was a betting woman, I'd give you ten to one that dear Milly's errand in coming here tonight was entirely her own idea.'

'I think you mean one hundred to one.' Flora smiled, although she felt stunned. She had no idea her father's books were worth so much — £1000! It was unbelievable. She shook her head. 'I think Milly's figure is a wild exaggeration. My father could never have owned books worth £1000!'

Startling News

Flora watched the small card being placed in Lambies' shop window on Wednesday morning — *Message boy wanted. Must be honest, smart, and hardworking. Apply within — to Miss Rennie at cake counter.*

The positions were much sought after, so within an hour, fourteen-year-old boys were being brought in by parents and some came themselves. Flora's heart ached at the desperate way in which they applied to her aunt.

Flora thought most of the boys would suit, but Aunt Isa had not singled one out. Now, at Thursday lunchtime, she saw another young lad arrive, followed by a tall woman wrapped in a heavy tartan shawl. The boy wore the unmistakable parish clothes issued by the local authorities for the children of the very poor; the shapeless, short-trousered, rough tweed suit, the black jumper with red bands through the collar, and matching heavy socks and hob-nailed boots.

Flora gulped audibly as she recognised the woman in the shawl as Mrs McNeill, who used to clean out Willie Young's newsagents' shop. The woman led the boy in, one arm round his shoulder, a mixture of fear and defiance on her face.

'You're looking well, Flora,' she said in the soft accent of one whose first language is Gaelic. 'I was hearing there was a job here which the boy could do. Could I be speaking with this Miss Rennie, please?'

'She's due back from lunch . . . ' Flora started as her aunt came through the front door.

Isa's eyebrows rose at the odd couple standing at her kiosk. In the mid-nineteen-thirties it was usually only poor, old women who still wore the shawl, and they were never customers in Lambies' High Class Provision merchants.

'This is another boy and his mother for an interview,' Flora said, as Mrs McNeill turned to face Aunt Isa and spoke her piece quickly. It sounded well rehearsed.

'My name is Catriona McNeill — this is my son, Roderick McNeill, who is honest and will work hard. He doesn't have references, but I have. I was a lady's maid to Lady Angusina Robertson.' She brought an envelope from under her shawl and held it out to Isa.

'And here are his father's references,' she said, adding several other papers.

Isa Rennie took them with an exclamation, for she hadn't had time to take off her coat. With a loud, long-suffering sigh she came round into the kiosk and opened up the papers.

She examined them one by one, becoming more and more still as she read them through.

She asked the boy the usual questions, and he answered in a polite West of Scotland accent, very different from his mother's soft Highland tones.

Isa stared at the two of them through her spectacles for a long moment. She saw the signs of malnutrition on both their faces, but also noticed they were scrubbed clean, and their clothes, although poor, were neatly brushed and obviously well-cared for.

'Your husband? What does he do now?' Isa asked coolly.

'He's unemployed. Lost his right arm in the war. But he's taught himself to write with his left hand,' Mrs McNeill answered, bringing out a carefully-folded page from a school jotter, and passed it over the counter.

'This is copper-plate writing!' Isa frowned, and looked suspicious.

'Yes.' Mrs McNeill gave a dispirited shrug. 'He thought he might get a job as a clerk. But there's plenty of able-bodied ones for any jobs that are going.'

Isa bent under the counter to her handbag and, after much fumbling, brought out an envelope. She scribbled on it.

'Take this to Mr Shiach at that address. He'll kit the boy out for work. Then come back here to meet Mr Campbell, who'll detail his duties. The wage is ten shillings a week and he'll get tips. From them he'll pay back this pound at sixpence a week.' Isa indicated the envelope.

Mrs McNeill took it, her face solemn, but her voice was husky.

'Thank you. Roddy won't let you down. It's a big honour to get work here. Even if he doesn't get kept on after sixteen, having worked with Lambies' makes it easier to get an apprenticeship . . . '

'Yes, yes . . . Now off you go — both of you. I have a lot of work to do,' Isa said, and turned away.

The mother and son walked out of the shop smiling, but several of the customers looked askance at a 'shawlie wife' being in Lambies'.

Flora saw the tears in Aunt Isa's eyes. ''A land fit for heroes to live in',' she murmured, when she realised Flora had noticed, 'that's what those men were promised.' She shoved the jotter paper in front of Flora. On it the boy's name, address, and age were written in perfect handwriting.

But what really filled Isa's mind was that the woman could have been herself. Lady's maids were always the most refined of the girls in service . . . and the husband was a joiner to trade — as was Isa's fiancé, dead in France. She turned away, biting her lip, and started to rearrange the display.

Flora felt a little chastened. She had begun to think her aunt liked the feeling of power being an interviewer gave. But she saw the stern front was only assumed. It was not part of Aunt Isa's duties to advance money for the boy's working clothes.

Just then Mona hurried in, her eyes wide with excitement. She carried a large, slim, boxed parcel and stopped at the kiosk for a moment.

'Bought a new dress for tomorrow night — Bartie is taking us to the Hotel du Ville. And that deserved a proper dinner gown . . . ' She hurried off.

Flora could hardly believe it — Mona buying another dress! She had dozens which she had rarely, if ever, worn. Then Flora became alarmed. The Hotel du Ville was the most exclusive restaurant in Glasgow, the place where visiting Royalty dined — even she knew that. But did Bartie?

She waylaid him a little later as he was making a delivery and voiced her anxiety.

'Now stop worrying!' He laughed heartily. 'I know exactly what I'm doing, escorting two fine young ladies there. Can't come soon enough for me!'

* * *

Customers were crowding the kiosk and she had no time to dwell further on the dinner-date she and Mona were to have with him next evening.

Then, in a lull between customers, Flora saw Mrs McNeill and her son return. He was wearing a fine, brown tweed knickerbocker suit with matching cap. They were of a style which had gone out twenty years previously, yet somehow on Roderick they looked exactly right. He was tall for a fourteen-year-old, and held himself well.

'That's a good outfit for riding a message bike,' Aunt Isa remarked briskly, coming out from the kiosk. She took the boy off to the back shop and Mrs McNeill stood and waited.

'How did you hear about the job?' Flora asked conversationally.

Govan, where Mrs McNeill lived, was miles away from this branch of Lambies' in Crosshill.

'Willie Young! Didn't you tell him about it?' Mrs McNeill answered, as if Flora should have realised.

'I . . . I . . . told him? *Me!*' Flora

gasped. 'I haven't spoken to Willie for weeks.'

Mrs McNeill looked at Flora curiously. 'Well, he's saying he sees you here nearly every day, and that you're to be wedded once a decent period of mourning for your father has passed.'

'No ... no ... ' Flora whispered through white lips. 'I'm not marrying Willie Young. He's got no right to say such things!'

'I'm very glad to hear it,' Mrs McNeill murmured. 'He is not a nice man, and I wouldn't work for him if I could get something better. But my husband doesn't keep well, and it's three shillings and sixpence at least every week for the doctor's visit, and there's medicine to be got as well. That Willie Young knows it and has me working hours past what he pays me for.'

'When ... who is he saying these things to?' Flora asked, trying to control her trembling.

'Everybody! He's even been to

jewellers to examine engagement rings,' Mrs McNeill answered. 'Tells everyone about all the fine clothes you wear now and your hair-do. You had that dress on yesterday.' Mrs McNeill pointed. 'He described it to a whole shop full of people.'

A customer came in and Flora had to break off the conversation to serve. She smiled and spoke automatically, but could not stop her hands trembling. Inside she was numbed at the thought of the podgy fifty-year-old putting out these stories. And that he should know about her hair and clothes meant he was spying on her. She'd only had her hair done on Tuesday at Aunt Isa's hairdresser.

That evening her aunt was quiet and preoccupied with her own thoughts and Flora felt unable to voice her horror at Willie Young's activities. Her mind thrashed back and forth over them. It was like a nightmare.

By suppertime, however, Flora had calmed down sufficiently to tell her aunt about Willie Young.

Aunt Isa listened, her mouth open in amazement. She made Flora repeat the story several times as if she could not take it in.

'But — but he must be stopped!' she exclaimed, pursing her lips and frowning.

'Yet Mrs McNeill will tell people the truth, and maybe if we see young Dr Anderson he might have a quiet word with Mr Willie Young, too . . . '

But Flora shrank from contacting Ralph Anderson.

★   ★   ★

Friday was always a busy day in Lambies', as housewives stocked up for the weekend. It was the day when most orders were either phoned into the office or brought by young maids from the big houses around Queen's Park.

Flora could recognise them now in their morning uniforms of heavy striped dresses and aprons with matching mob caps on their heads. Some of them imperiously complained if they were kept waiting, and she soon recognised there was a kind of aristocracy among them, linked with the status of their employers.

It made her understand Mrs McLaurin's attitudes — her first mistress coming from 'titled stock.'

A special delivery of hand-made Easter eggs arrived, and Isa Rennie groaned as she looked round her tastefully-displayed merchandise. There wasn't a vacant space, so one would have to be made quickly. Then Mr Campbell brought out a long list of orders, and laid it on the counter with his usual clicking of heels and bows.

'Required as soon as possible!' he said crisply.

Isa quickly put a number against each item and passed the list to Flora.

'Get these ready in that order, and take them through to Mr Campbell when you have a minute.'

Flora was delighted to be entrusted

with this task, as Aunt Isa usually attended to orders herself.

One of the first was for Mona's stepmother. Its varied contents made Flora think that Nadia must still be unwell, and wondered if Ralph Anderson had been contacted for medical help yet.

The little trips to the bustling back shop were a novelty — overseeing that each of her parcels and fancy cake boxes was placed carefully on top of their respective orders.

Mona looked down from the little glass-sided office and saw Flora, busy at the orders. She pushed back the sliding window and called to Flora.

'I'm going to change into my glad rags up here when the shop closes. Why don't you do the same? Mr Lambie says it's all right!' she shouted down cheerfully.

'I'll go home at lunch-time and get my things,' Flora agreed. She still wasn't sure whether she was looking forward to this evening out or dreading it. It was so entirely outwith any experience she had ever had and, despite Bartie's assurances, she was anxious about the cost and grandeur.

That morning she didn't take a tea break but worked through, finishing all the orders as well as attending to the counter while Aunt Isa built up a marvellous display of Easter eggs.

At noon Flora hurried out of the shop and ran along to Allison Street to catch a tram to Shawlands. At the stop she was almost rooted to the ground in horror as she saw Willie Young in the long line of people who got off the tram.

Flora shrank behind a tall man waiting to board in front of her, and Willie brushed past without noticing. She had little doubt of where he was going, for at this time she was usually in the kiosk on her own while Aunt Isa had lunch. This must be when he spied on her.

Mona came clattering down the short flight of wooden steps from the office, when Flora returned with her clothes.

'Decided you can't wear that jacket with your new dress, so I've brought in a little black edge-to-edge fur jacket . . . ' Mona chattered happily on, pointing to the dark tweed, three-quarter jacket Flora had first worn for her interview, the only presentable coat she possessed.

Flora tried to tell Mona about Willie Young, but the younger girl dismissed him as a stupid crank, and was more anxious to discuss their joint date tonight with Bartie Darroch. But when Flora got to the kiosk Aunt Isa had seen Willie Young, too.

'I was with a customer, but I threw him such a look to show my annoyance. He disappeared after that. Dick and Harry on the ham counter raised their fists to him.'

Aunt Isa tried to sound disapproving of the two young men, but a certain admiration for their chivalry coloured her voice.

Flora felt better now she was back in

the shop, and somehow secure, knowing so many were looking out for her interests.

The date with Bartie Darroch obviously interested the whole staff. Even old Mr Barclay, the cashier, stopped at the kiosk at 7.30, beaming.

'My office has to become a changing room for young ladies, so I must be a gentleman and vacate it.' He smiled with old-fashioned courtesy, as he paused to chat with Aunt Isa while Flora took her things and hurried up the wooden steps to the office.

Mona had already changed into the new royal blue velvet dress with a long string of pearls over the swathed front. The white fur evening cape draped over her shoulders toned with her blonde hair, and gave her an almost ethereal look.

*   *   *

It only took Flora moments to change and she felt a shiver of excitement. She had never worn a dress and bolero like this before, and its well-cut lines showed off her figure to advantage.

The pleated white jabot and cuffs relieved the stark black, and gave her face a luminous quality.

'Now sit down and I'll touch up your hair,' Mona commanded. Then she brought out her make-up case and, overruling Flora's doubts, deftly creamed, powdered, and lipsticked her face.

'There!' Mona stood back, smiling with pleasure at her own skill. 'Been dying to do that to you. You'll have every head turning.'

The only mirror was above Mr Barclay's seat to give him a view of what was going on in the back shop, and she knelt on his chair and manoeuvred it so that Flora could see her handiwork.

'Oh, Mona, you're a genius!' Flora patted her hair, and stared at her graceful figure in the mirror. She felt a rush of gratitude towards her friend.

Mona helped Flora into the fur jacket and squealed happily at the result.

Flora stroked the smooth black fur. 'It's lovely . . . but at the moment I can't afford three pounds.' She made to take it off.

'Rubbish!' Mona caught the lapels and pulled the jacket back on. 'Pay me half a crown a week, when you can.' And before Flora could object further she was out of the office and clattering down the steps to greet Bartie.

In the mirror Flora again admired herself in the jacket. She'd always longed to have one just like it. And £3 was a ridiculous price. It was worth more. Yet, she only earned 30/- a week and already owed Aunt Isa two weeks' lodgings, through buying other things from Mona.

But just then Aunt Isa came up into the office and gasped.

'Oh, Flora — you look like royalty!' This was the highest compliment Aunt Isa could give. She always knew with a little attention her niece could be truly eye-catching.

Bartie had arrived, looking tall and splendid in a heavy black coat with a velvet collar, over his dinner suit. On his head he wore one of the fashionable homburg hats. He was in a happy mood, anxious to show everyone his new Morris Seven car which had just cost him £120.

It seemed all the staff, even Mr Lambie, came outside and waved them off in it. Flora sat quietly in the back seat, while Mona was in front chattering to Bartie. Mona was knowledgeable about cars and could discuss all the different points, while Flora just savoured the fact that she was actually riding in one. Nobody she knew in Partick possessed one.

At the Hotel du Ville restaurant, Mona was in her element renewing the acquaintance of Louis, the bowing head waiter. Flora waited quietly as Mona exchanged banter with him. Her heart thumped with trepidation and she hoped that she would know how to act in this ultra-sophisticated place.

They left their coats in the softly-lit powder room, and Bartie proudly escorted them into the thickly-carpeted restaurant, where a trio played on a little flower-bedecked balcony high up on the wall, at the farthest end.

'Ah! Hello, Dad!' Bartie suddenly stopped at a table where an older man sat with two matronly ladies. 'Hello, Mama, Aunt Maisie . . . ' Bartie nodded, then turned to introduce his two guests, not noticing that Mona had stiffened.

Flora smiled and shook hands with them, murmuring the usual pleasant-ries. Then Mona, unsmiling, shook hands with Bartie's parents.

'Oh, we know one another,' Bartie's Aunt Maisie said dryly, nodding coolly in Mona's direction. Both seemed to studiously avoid shaking hands. 'My son will soon be joining us,' she added meaningfully.

'I do hope you have a pleasant meal,'

Mona said, formally polite, and turned to Bartie. 'Where's our table? I'm ravenous!'

Soon the three of them were settled at a table under the balcony.

Mona hid her face behind the large menu which the head waiter had given each of them. She felt like screaming. Why hadn't she realised there was a connection between Bartie and Hamish? It was frustrating. She'd cut all ties with the old crowd and started her life afresh with new friends — yet here was Hamish back in her life.

The menu seemed very complicated to Flora, but Bartie made it easy to choose, by pointing out the different dishes to order. He was no stranger to this place, Flora thought wryly. And to think she had worried about it being too expensive!

The food was delicious and Flora was able to relax and look around at all the beautifully-dressed women. It was a far cry from Partick, where the unemployed stood on each corner, huddled against the wind. Then her gaze fell on Bartie's parents, and she blinked as she saw Hamish Buchanan sitting with them. He smiled and got up.

'Here's my cousin Hamish!' Bartie exclaimed. 'He's a lawyer.'

Hamish, distinguished looking in his dinner suit, made his way over.

'Ah, yes, I used to know him rather well,' Mona murmured as he came up to the table.

'Hello, Mona, good evening, Flora.' Hamish nodded to the young women.

'The two bonniest girls in Glasgow and trust you to know them already!' Bartie grumbled good-naturedly. 'Thought I'd made you jealous in my choice of company.'

'I'm very impressed.' Hamish smiled.

'Sit down and join us for coffee,' Bartie offered.

As Hamish joined them, Flora suddenly realised why Mona was so distant with Bartie's Aunt Maisie. She was Hamish's mother — the woman who'd phoned Mona after her father's disappearance to break off the romance with her son.

'Hamish!' Mona cried in a bright voice. 'Flora could do with some legal advice — how to stop a persistent admirer telling everyone that she's agreed to marry him.'

Flora was flustered that her hidden dread was to be the subject of a light conversation. Bartie was immediately eager to hear the details, so Mona luridly described Willie's unsavoury appearance and his furtive spying from outside the shop.

But Hamish came to Flora's aid at once. 'This kind of thing can be amusing for onlookers, but very trying for the person involved,' he said.

'Yes, but I don't feel it's time for legal action yet,' Flora murmured. 'My aunt believes that it will soon be known that I never accepted his proposal. He'll be ridiculed and it'll die away.'

Hamish thought this a sensible attitude. He seemed so genuinely interested that Flora found she could talk easily with him.

Then the subject changed as Bartie spoke proudly of his growing success in business.

When it came time to leave Mona passed over her cloakroom token to Flora. 'Be a darling and collect the coats!' she said, and turned back to continue her chat with the two men.

★ ★ ★

Flora got up and made her way through the restaurant to the ladies' powder room. She noticed the table where Bartie's parents and aunt had sat was empty.

In the powder room, as she went to collect the coats, she overheard the conversation of two women with their backs to her — one of them was Hamish's mother.

' . . . I told the girl he'd just finished paying back his uncle for putting him through university and was in no position to take on a wife like her,' she said. 'Hamish was furious with me for interfering, but I thought it only fair that the girl should know his position . . .'

Hamish's mother turned and saw Flora.

'Oh, yes, you're the girl who has just lost her father. My son told me about you. I'm sorry about your loss.'

The girl attendant passed the furs over to Flora then and Mrs Buchanan's hand touched the black jacket gently.

'Sable! My, my! You're well off,' she murmured dryly and, unabashed, turned back to continue her conversation.

Out in the foyer, Flora met up with the other three. Bartie drove the two girls home and dropped them at the close in Shawlands. He declined their offer of tea as he had an early job in the morning.

Flora and Mona stopped on the landing outside their doors to have a private post-mortem, but when Flora tried to bring up the subject of the jacket, Mona brushed it aside.

'Oh, no! Not tonight! We'll discuss it some other time.' She was more anxious to go over the meal, music and company — although she was noncommittal about the unexpected appearance of Hamish Buchanan.

'Bartie must have known his father and mother were going to be at the Hotel du Ville tonight. He used us like a couple of trophies to show his father his success in business . . . '

Suddenly, Aunt Isa's door opened. 'Mona, will you come in for a minute. Mrs McLaurin is here, and so is Dr Anderson. He . . . they . . . want to speak to you,' she said a little anxiously.

Mona exchanged a mystified glance with Flora and followed her into the living-room where Mrs McLaurin sat looking important.

'Mona, dearie, we've got news for you,' she began, 'and I thought it best that Dr Anderson should tell you himself . . . on, I may say, the instructions of your stepmother.

Mona looked sharply at Ralph Anderson, who raised a placating hand. 'I hope it's happy news. The coming of a new life should be — even if the mother is a trifle old for her first child.'

Mona sat down shakily in a chair as Ralph went on to reveal that her stepmother was several months pregnant.

'My . . . my father should know. We'll have to get word to him . . . surely the lawyer would have some contact?' Mona said quickly.

'Mrs Alexander, your stepmother, doesn't want him told till after the birth,' Mrs McLaurin murmured piously, thoroughly enjoying her rôle.

'Flora, make a cup of tea!' Aunt Isa said. She had just heard the news herself and was stunned, too.

Ralph saw what a bombshell his news had been, and went out of his way to be reassuring. 'My patient is a very healthy woman, and now she knows why she felt so strange, she is a very, very happy one, too!'

'It changes the situation — I'll really have to look after her. Your father would expect me to do it,' Mrs McLaurin said to Mona as they discussed this new development.

'You've changed so much,' Ralph said to Flora as she handed him a cup of tea. 'I hardly know this new person, so unlike the girl who used to give me cocoa when I was studying at her parents' fireside.'

She smiled quietly, knowing his memory would be of her in lumpy, hand-knitted jumpers, ill-fitting skirts and unstyled hair.

'I'm still the same person underneath. I still miss my father, and even my old home, at times.'

'Did you know your brother had your father's books valued, and that they might realise over a thousand pounds?' he asked.

'Yes, Milly came, looking to add to the collection that copy of Burns you returned to me. But I feel it's a bit soon after my father's death to discuss selling his books,' Flora said with uncharacteristic sharpness.

'Yes, I can understand how you must feel,' he said, then sighed. 'Maybe I'm a bit obsessed about the value of things at the moment. I'm trying to work out how to finance buying a practice . . . anyway, you won't have money worries now you intend marrying Willie . . . '

'Oh, no!' Flora's shriek was followed by total silence as everyone stared at her, amazed. 'I do not intend to marry that man — not now, nor ever!'

A Family Gathering

Friday might be the day for orders in Lambies', but Saturday was when personal shoppers packed the shop after Friday pay night.

Flora had no time to think about the previous evening at the Hotel du Ville as customers crowded round the kiosk, but any time her eye went to the glass-sided office above the wines and spirits at the end of the shop, she saw Mona looking bored and disgruntled.

For the past week Mona had been in high good humour, looking forward to the dinner date with Bartie. Now that had been and gone, she had nothing more to look forward to. And with the orders finished there was no urgent work, only bookkeeping, which gave her time to think — especially about her father's disappearance.

The crowds of customers had

thinned out by the time the afternoon tea-break came, and Flora was glad to sit down in the back shop and rest her feet. In moments Mona joined her.

'Loly is going back to live in the old house with Nadia.' Mona sighed, sipping her tea. 'Nadia would like me to go back too, but I don't want to leave the flat. It's so handy for getting here. And I've got to prove to myself that I can make a new life . . . '

'Hello!' Bartie's large figure suddenly appeared beside them, his sandy-coloured hair and face covered in coal dust. 'Pour me a cup of tea, please. I've been delivering anthracite for the boiler.'

At once Mona brightened. 'Flora's having lunch with her family down at Scotstoun tomorrow. She could do with a lift. And I'll come along for the ride, if you can do it!' she finished pertly.

'Mona!' Flora was aghast at her friend's impertinence. 'I always go by tram.'

'Not at all — my new car needs a drive.' Bartie brushed aside her objections and she sat helplessly as Bartie and Mona arranged for her to be picked up before noon next day.

'I'll bring a picnic and we could go a run down to Loch Lomond afterwards,' Mona suggested.

The proposal delighted Bartie. He drank his tea standing up, then was off to finish his delivery.

'I think Bartie's marvellous. He turns his hand to any kind of work,' Mona said, watching him go. 'He's going to succeed, and I want to be there when he does.'

Flora wondered exactly what her friend was implying. But she had no time to discuss it, her tea-break was over. And she'd been a few minutes late getting back to the kiosk at lunchtime after a confrontation with Mona, insisting she take back the fur jacket.

Now Flora knew it was sable she couldn't possibly accept it for a mere £3. Aunt Isa thought it was an asset

Mona could use if she was ever short of money and told her so.

At closing time Flora decided to buy a fancy cake to take to the family lunch the next day. She never went empty handed.

But Aunt Isa had a better idea. 'A nice sherry might be a more suitable gift. Make them realise you're not the self-effacing Flora of old. Mr Lambie keeps a fine cask of Spanish Amontillado.'

Flora liked the idea, if only to see Milly's face when she produced it. So she went to Mr Hugh, and he gave her one of his special sherries, bottled on the premises.

Aunt Isa examined it when they got home. 'I remember my mother always kept a bottle of this in the house, and when anyone special dropped in unexpectedly, they were given it in a crystal glass with some thin tea biscuits. I used to think it was so genteel.'

Flora wanted to hear more about her maternal grandmother because she was supposed to look very like her.

Instead she had to listen patiently to all the advice Aunt Isa gave her about the family lunch the following day.

'Now don't sit quietly and let them ride rough shod over you. Make sure you have a say in the selling of your father's books — for they *will* be sold. Remember — nostalgia is all very well, but your father's gone now, and a nice little nest egg of a few hundred pounds at your back will be very comforting.'

Flora knew her aunt was probably right. Aunt Isa had little time for sentiment where her father's books were concerned.

Next day Bartie came for her in his little car and Mona came down to it with a large wicker picnic basket. 'It's crammed with goodies!' she exclaimed. Flora wished she was joining them for the picnic. It was a gentle March day with very little wind, the sun warm and golden, heating the earth for the spring flowers.

She never looked forward to the

family lunches now as she did when her mother used to have them. Then she was busily occupied, helping with the cooking and serving. But since her sisters-in-law had taken over, she seemed just to sit dumbly as conversation went on above her head.

It was very comfortable and quick to travel by car. And in no time they were turning off Dumbarton Road down the avenues of terraced Victorian houses where her brother lived and had his dental practice.

Being Sunday, Scotstoun was unusually quiet. The clamour from the shipyards on the nearby Clyde was absent. And the dungaree-clad men who worked in them during the week were coming from church now, with their wives and families spruce in their Sunday-best clothes.

'This it?' Bartie asked, stopping at an end house with an extension at the side bearing a brass plate 'George Lochart — Dental Surgeon. Consultations by Appointment.'

Mona giggled. 'Looks as if you're the last to arrive. They're all standing at the window having a good look at us.'

Bartie got out and helped Flora from the car. 'We'll come back and collect you between four and five this afternoon,' he said, and was back in the driving seat before she had time to object.

Yet Flora was relieved. She didn't know how long this lunch would take with the inevitable discussion about the sale of her father's books. But their coming back would give her a definite excuse to leave.

*　*　*

Flora! You look marvellous!' Sally sang out as Flora came up the short garden path. 'It's a transformation — let's have a look at you!' she cried as she drew Flora into the house, holding her at arm's length, looking her over.

Flora smiled quietly, and was glad that she had on the dark tweed suit she'd worn for her interview. And her newly-done hair gave her extra confidence.

'Will you read us stories?' Jim and Rupert, her five-and eight-year-old nephews, clamoured at the sight of her.

'Maybe later!' she murmured, as Sally took her upstairs to take off her hat and coat.

'I just can't believe it!' Sally kept repeating as Flora took off her things and tidied her hair at the mirror. 'Going to live with your Aunt Isa was the best thing you could have done. You look stunning!'

Flora smiled at Sally's enthusiasm for her new appearance. She was grateful for the warm-hearted approval. And when she went into the front parlour, her two older brothers were gruffly pleased to see her.

'I told you she'd changed,' Milly said with a frosty smile as they remarked on how well she was looking.

Milly's eyebrows arched as Sally fetched glasses. 'I doubt if the old Flora would even have known what sherry was!' She sniffed.

'She's learnt quickly, then!' Sally held her glass high in a toasting gesture, then took an appreciative sip.

Sally was easy-going and sometimes her meals were poor, but today Flora thought she had surpassed herself — until Sally admitted that her new daily help had been a cook, and she'd come in specially to prepare the meal for today.

Of her two sisters-in-law, Flora liked Sally best. She was honest and kind hearted, although tending to self-indulgence. And Flora knew that sometimes these extravagances caused trouble between husband and wife.

On the other hand Milly was a superlative housewife. Her home, a flat above the bank where she and Robert had lived since they were married, was uncluttered and well run.

After the meal when they retired to the parlour again, the atmosphere was somewhat relaxed. They had all come to accept this new Flora. But she steeled herself, waiting for the discussion on the books, which came almost immediately.

'Flora, I believe you know that Robert had father's books valued by an antique dealer,' George said bluntly. 'And his first estimate was around the £1000 mark. Now he says he has an American collector who is interested. He'll give £1500, if he can have a quick sale.'

'I didn't know about the second offer,' Flora murmured, still trying to come to terms with the fact that her father's beloved books would be sold.

Their faces showed they had already decided.

'It's hardly been any time since the funeral. Do we have to talk about selling the books . . . ?' she faltered.

'It's all very well for you, for money will soon be no problem,' Milly said shrilly. 'But from our share Robert and I could buy a lovely little bungalow in Bearsden or Clarkston. And I know

George is keen to get some modern equipment for his practice.'

Flora gazed at her, anger growing at this outburst. 'What do you mean — money being no problem? I hope it's not what I suspect?' she said coldly.

Milly gaped. Flora had never used such a tone to her before.

★   ★   ★

'Well, I heard that you've agreed to marry Willie Young . . . ' she stammered.

'I haven't!' Flora answered in a controlled voice.

'Well, it all seems very strange . . . all these expensive new clothes, and the new hairdo,' Milly blustered.

Flora almost felt sorry for her. She had a talent for saying the wrong things.

'They're second hand!' she answered simply.

Robert stood up and frowned at his wife, who was about to try to justify herself again.

'Flora, let's get this straight. You've not accepted Willie Young's proposal, yet he's told the world and his wife that you have?'

'If I intended getting married, don't you think you would have been one of the first to know?' Flora sighed, thoroughly disgruntled that this matter had come up again.

'Indeed!' Robert announced firmly. 'As the eldest of the family, I'll make a point of meeting Mr Young and making your decision clear to him. It's gone far enough — people have been coming into the bank talking as if it is a fait accompli!'

'Very well, if you think that will finish it.' Flora shrugged. The subject nauseated her.

She was glad when they returned to discussing the sale of the books, and surprised herself by coolly suggesting that the matter be put into the hands of a lawyer, as Aunt Isa had advised her.

Robert and George thought this was unnecessary, but when they saw she was determined, they agreed. By this time Sally was becoming bored with the discussion.

'Let Flora fix up a lawyer to take overall charge. Maybe even see that everything is above board. After all, the dealer might be a little sticky fingered,' Sally suggested.

Flora was taken off guard, she hadn't thought she would be put on the spot to supply a lawyer. But she saw the smirk on Milly's face at her consternation, and took control of the situation.

'Yes, I do know a lawyer who is a partner in an old-established law firm — Hamish Buchanan of McEwen, McMorrin and Souter.'

'All right,' George nodded. 'I've heard of them — a good firm.'

'Had you included in the collection the copy of Burns' poems I have?' Flora asked. She saw at once by her brothers' faces that they did not know about the book which Ralph Anderson had returned to her, so she explained the circumstances.

'I — I think Flora should keep that book,' Milly put in quickly. 'It's of great sentimental value to her, and the only thing she has belonging to her father.'

George and Robert exchanged glances. 'I don't mind!' George shrugged.

'Yes, that would be a fair solution!' Robert nodded.

Flora felt a great weight lifted from her. She had dreaded any wrangling over her father's books, and she would never sell his little book of poetry. Yet Milly's gesture surprised her — did she have second thoughts and regret coming to ask for it — or was she afraid the others would find out she had?

After coffee Flora went into the kitchen to help wash up, and Milly joined her. Sally, who had provided the meal, stayed in the lounge with the two brothers.

Flora was surprised to see that Milly was now full of suppressed excitement.

'£1500 means we'll get at least £400 each, after all expenses are paid,' she said. 'It's unbelievable! Now Robert and I can buy a house and get away from living above the bank.

'They've got used to him always being there at their beck and call, phoning him to get documents and what-not when the bank is closed. When promotion comes up he's over-looked . . . he's just too useful where he is . . . I'm positive his name doesn't get put forward.'

'Thought I'd come and supervise,' Sally interrupted. 'And I want to get away from my husband describing to Robert the new electric drill, chair and light he'll buy with this windfall. Thinks it'll double his patients.' she turned to Flora. 'What are you going to do with your money — any plans?'

Flora paused, her hands in the suds, and shook her head. She had no idea.

'I haven't given it any thought,' she told them.

'Better watch out,' Milly smirked. 'When you're worth a few hundred pounds, maybe Ralph Anderson will want to get to know you better. Young doctors need to marry girls with nest-eggs.'

Flora turned back to the sink. Milly had done it again — destroyed all warmth between them.

For the rest of the time Flora read to the boys, and her young nieces, Cherry and Millicent, joined them too. Sally had often called on her to baby-sit, but Milly never did, so Flora didn't know her nieces as well as her nephews. They seemed very observant little girls, but solemnly old fashioned for six and seven-year-olds.

Promptly, at four o'clock, Bartie's little square-shaped Morris Seven drew up at the gate.

Minutes later Sally brought Bartie and Mona into the parlour and the atmosphere brightened immediately with their presence.

But the two little girls stayed at the window, staring out at the car.

Bartie soon noticed and bent down to them.

'Do you like it? It's new!'

'It's nice and shiny,' Millicent assured him solemnly.

'But it doesn't fit you,' Cherry said seriously. 'You need a bigger one.'

Bartie laughed uproariously, although Milly was covered in confusion that her daughter might have been rude.

'You're right!' Bartie agreed with the child. 'But in a year or two, when I've made some more money, I'll give that one to my wife and get myself a bigger one.'

'But first of all he'll have to find a wife!' Mona quipped.

'Ah, but I've one in mind, if she'll have me.' Bartie grinned, and looked directly at Flora, giving her a huge wink.

Flora smiled, treating his remark as mere light-hearted banter, but her smile faded when for a fleeting second she saw hurt on Mona's face.

At once Flora wondered if her friend's regard for Bartie might go deeper than she'd realised.

After all, Mona had sought out his

company at every opportunity. Somehow, Flora found the matter disturbing.

'My, my! Who would have thought our Flora, who was a real little dormouse, would have suitors lining up now?' Milly simpered.

Robert glared at his wife. 'Flora, we'll leave you to contact the lawyer. Keep us informed,' he said quietly.

★   ★   ★

Next day Flora wondered if she had imagined the look of hurt on Mona's face, for on the journey home and since, she'd been her usual blithe self.

That afternoon, Nadia Alexander, Mona's stepmother, came into the shop. She was still pale but Flora was glad to see she looked more rested now and much brighter.

Nadia asked specially for Flora to attend her. This meant going round the whole shop and serving all her needs at each counter. It was the first time Flora had done it, for Aunt Isa usually attended account customers who asked for this service.

'You'll have heard my news,' Nadia said at once, and Flora nodded carefully, as she scooped sugar from a large canvas sack into a stiff brown paper bag.

'I can't believe I'm so lucky. I really thought I was dying . . . ' Nadia was eager to talk about her present state of health.

Flora only half listened as she filled bags, and fetched and carried goods to add to the pile in front of her. She already knew all Nadia's reactions from Mrs McLaurin's nightly news. But Nadia's final words caught her full attention.

' . . . so that is why I want you to persuade Mona to come back home.'

Flora murmured a non-committal reply, for she didn't want to take sides in this family affair. Watching Aunt Isa in such situations had taught her this kind of diplomacy.

'You see, Dr Anderson can't really

tell exactly when the baby will come,' Nadia explained. 'Mona is like a daughter to me and I want her near when the time comes. After all, it will be her little brother or sister . . . '

'Well, hello, Nadia.' A matronly woman interrupted.

Flora swallowed as she saw it was Hamish Buchanan's mother. She bent her head over the list of groceries and totalled it up while the two women discussed the coming baby.

'Just hope it's a boy — that will soon bring that husband of yours back from his wanderings.' Mrs Buchanan sniffed. 'Ridiculous that when his business hits a bad patch, he just ups and offs, leaving his responsibilities.'

'Oh, no!' Nadia sighed. 'I didn't support him — he tried to discuss matters with me, but I was feeling so wretched that I didn't listen. And when he persisted . . . I — I told him I was sorry I'd married him . . . '

Hearing the intimate details of Nadia's marriage embarrassed Flora.

But Mrs Buchanan was not very interested in Nadia's long-winded explanations and her eyes fastened on Flora.

'You're the girl with the sable jacket!'

'I just had it for the evening,' Flora murmured.

'I see.' Mrs Buchanan nodded, and stared hard at Flora, assessing her. 'Yes, my son said you were a sensible kind of lassie.'

Flora smiled politely, wondering if Hamish Buchanan would tell his mother she had arranged an appointment with him.

Mona had helped her to use the phone today at lunchtime, and coached her on how to call the exchange to be put through to the office switchboard, then to ask for Hamish.

It had been a frightening, heart-palpitating new experience.

★   ★   ★

Now she checked her list, tapping with the end of the pencil the items in the

126

pile before her, then passed the bill to Nadia, who continued talking about her husband. All the time Flora was very aware of Mrs Buchanan's continued scrutiny.

Then Mr Campbell came from the back shop and with important flourishes packed Nadia's goods, which he would send immediately to her home by an errand boy.

'Now remember, Flora, try to get Mona to come home. She'll listen to you,' Nadia said in parting.

'Hmm! You'll be the first that girl has ever listened to, then,' Mrs Buchanan said dryly. 'And now, m'dear, you can attend to me in the same way.'

Only account customers were given this treatment and Mrs Buchanan wasn't even a regular visitor to Lambies'.

Flora looked at Aunt Isa for guidance and she gave a small nod of assent.

By the time Mrs Buchanan's purchases were at the tallying stage, Flora felt almost dazed, answering her searching questions. They were brusquely direct and difficult to evade.

Aunt Isa was annoyed when she returned to the kiosk.

'Dreadful type who thinks because we are serving, that they have the right to know all our personal history. And she'd be aware that only special customers get . . . ' She stopped in mid-sentence.

A sudden thumping noise erupted from the back shop, with bottles falling and angry voices. Mr Lambie was out, so Aunt Isa hurried through and found the tweed-clad figure of Roderick McNeill kneeling astride Jamie Morton, the top message boy.

Jamie was struggling and bellowing as his outstretched hands were held to the floor.

Mr Campbell was shouting orders to stop which the boys ignored. But Aunt Isa's prim outraged tones demanding an explanation had them scrambling to their feet in moments.

Both boys stood silently before her. The unwritten code of boys' honour demanded neither of them would 'clipe' on the other; although the fear of repercussions had started to show on both faces.

'I'll tell you what happened!' Mona called down from the open window of the office. 'One of the new boy's initiation japes went too far. A crate of empty bottles was pushed into his path as he was carrying his first order to his bike — the tyres had already been let down twice.'

'These stupid pranks on new boys must stop!' Aunt Isa rounded on Jamie Morton. 'There could have been a serious accident. And you, Roderick McNeill, must learn to work with people without losing your temper. Get back to work, the pair of you, and if Mr Campbell has to report either of you again, this incident will count against you.'

Mr Campbell was gratified to have his authority recognised.

'Yes, indeed! My eye will be on them from now on,' he assured Isa Rennie, fixing the two boys with what he thought was his fierce look.

When Tom, Dick and Harry on the ham counter heard the outcome of the altercation they were flabbergasted.

'The Dragon is losing her touch,' Tom marvelled. 'She'd have had us frog-marched out of the shop for half of that!'

Later that evening, as Flora and Mona were together in Mona's flat deciding what Flora would wear for her appointment with Hamish Buchanan, Mona brought the subject up again.

'I'm glad your aunt didn't report those boys to Mr Hugh. The other boys were making fun of that old-fashioned suit the new boy was wearing — looks ridiculous! The kind of thing my father wore as a boy.'

'He's got nothing else to wear,' Flora answered and explained about Roderick's sad home circumstances.

Mona was appalled, especially when she learned his mother was also being cheated in her employment by Willie Young.

'How terrible!' she exclaimed. Then she paused, her face brightening. 'I'll employ her here — a few hours every day to clean the place and lay the fire — maybe even prepare a meal — do you think she'd be interested?'

'It's possible!' Flora said slowly, knowing that Mona could afford to. She had an extra weekly allowance from her father, besides her salary.

Flora's eye travelled round the cold, neglected room. 'You certainly need someone to help, now Mrs McLaurin is going back to Nadia.'

'Good, we'll go and see her tomorrow after your interview with Hamish,' Mona decided, then added dryly, 'Wonder if his mother will be standing behind his shoulder?'

She saw Flora looked puzzled.

'She pokes her nose in everywhere. Didn't I see her in the shop this afternoon looking you over? Her nephew Bartie has no doubt been singing your praises and so she'd want to see you for herself.'

'Me! You're exaggerating!' Flora gave an incredulous laugh.

Mona looked at her friend pityingly. 'Never knew anyone with such a low opinion of themselves. Don't you ever look in the mirror?'

Flora looked away, confused.

Too Impulsive

Next afternoon, when they left the shop for their half-day off, Mona and Flora set off into town by tram. Flora was quiet and tense, anxious about her first interview with a solicitor, even if it was Hamish Buchanan, who had treated her kindly.

They got off the tram in Sauchiehall Street and walked to the office in Bath Street. Mona opened the half-glazed door and they went into a small, gloomy space, a wooden counter and glass partition barring their way. She struck the little rounded brass bell on the counter.

The window was pulled back and a small bald-headed man with a pen holder behind his ear stared at them.

'Mr . . . Mr Buchanan, please!' Flora murmured after Mona had nudged her forward.

'What's your name and I'll see if he's in?' came the curt reply.

'It's Miss Flora Lochart — and she has an appointment!' Mona said with an edge to her voice.

The little man disappeared, closing the window with a slam, leaving them in semi-darkness again.

After a few moments a door opened nearby and the area was flooded with light from within as Hamish Buchanan greeted them.

'Hello, Hamish, I'm here merely as Flora's companion. So be a darling while you're doing the legal bit, and arrange some tea and a magazine for me,' Mona announced as they went into the cluttered outer office, where papers and files were stacked on every surface. The heads of the staff appeared above them as they worked at their desks.

Hamish settled Mona in a chair and arranged that tea be brought to her and also to his office for himself and Flora.

Flora was surprised to find Hamish's

office almost Spartan in its neatness after the seeming chaos of the outer office.

A comforting fire burned in an old-fashioned barred grate and his desk was over by a window which looked out on the backs of other buildings.

He saw her glance and smiled. 'I'm just the junior partner and don't merit a view, but there's a good fire here, so let's sit down by it and discuss your business.'

Sitting in a small armchair by the fire put Flora at ease, and all her worry and tension about this interview disappeared. She found she was able to state quite simply the details of the offer for her father's books.

Hamish listened carefully and then started to explain the legalities involved in a deceased's estate. Flora tried to concentrate on his words but was soon lost.

He noticed her discomfort and stopped with a smile. 'I'll not bore you with the technicalities. The case is quite simple. Your brother probably knows the book agent's reputation through the bank, but I'll check things out and get back to you as soon as I can.'

The business part of the interview was all but over when the tea tray was brought by the little bald man.

'Well, well, we are honoured,' Hamish exclaimed, turning to Flora. 'This is Hodges, our head clerk. He started with the firm fifty years ago. Hodges knows everything about the law. And his deeds are a work of art.' Hamish tapped a hand-written parchment.

Flora admired the faultless writing, and put her hand out politely. 'How do you do, Mr Hodges? You're certainly a perfectionist.'

On his way out, Hodges paused at the door and winked cheekily at Hamish. 'Ay, but two such bonnie lassies — it'll be difficult to choose!' And with a dry chuckle he left them.

As they left the lawyer's office, Flora wondered if Mona still felt something for Hamish. Had she assumed that strident liveliness in his office just now to hide it?

Flora was tempted to enquire discreetly, but as they reached the street, rain was lashing down. They had to battle against it under their separate umbrellas to reach the Subway in Buchanan Street.

The Subway was being modernised, with upholstered seating replacing the slatted wooden side benches, and the increased lighting making it more comfortable. It was a familiar form of travelling for Flora, but this was the first time Mona had used it and it seemed to reverse their roles.

It was Flora who led the way now as they descended to the platform and a blast of damp air with a unique, yet not unpleasant, odour hit them.

'That's the famous Subway smell.' Flora smiled and explained that the old cable system had been scrapped and the whole circuit would be electrified by the end of the month. 'But they'll still be noisy and as shoogly as before!'

Flora laughed. 'Then I hear it's to be re-named the Underground — but I think Glasgow folk will always call it the Subway.'

★   ★   ★

Flora knew Govan well. When her parents were alive she often got the special halfpenny fare on the Subway from Merkland Street station and travelled the few minutes under the Clyde to the shops on the other side of the river in Govan.

As in Partick, the unemployed, wearing shabby flat caps, stood at corners, shoulders hunched and hands in pockets. And down side streets, groups of women stood chatting at closes, wrapped in shawls, some with babies cradled in the folds.

They turned to watch as the two fashionably-dressed young women passed them.

Flora led Mona to the street near Harmony Row where the McNeills lived. Soon they were climbing the pipe-clayed stairs to the third floor of the gloomy tenement.

'Mrs McNeill is . . . ' Flora paused, and then went on tentatively, 'a strangely independent kind of person . . . and will be wary of a stranger. Will I do the talking?'

'Do you mean she might refuse?' Mona said in surprise.

'No . . . I don't think so . . . ' Flora floundered a little. It was difficult to exactly predict how Catriona McNeill would react, but she sensed that it might not be in the way Mona expected.

'All right!' Mona shrugged. 'If you think it's best.'

On the top landing a roof fanlight made it brighter and they stopped at the middle door and knocked. A small girl of about nine opened it and peeped out. Flora asked for her mother and without a word the door was closed.

'What do we do now?' Mona asked, baffled.

'Just wait — Mrs McNeill will be here in a moment.'

At that, the unsmiling figure of Mrs McNeill stepped out on to the door mat and closed the door behind her.

'So it is you, Flora Lochart. I am pleased to see you looking so well,' she said politely, in her soft, lilting accent.

Flora introduced Mona and without any further preamble stated their reason for coming.

Mrs McNeill's face did not soften. She looked from one to the other and sighed.

'It is a very good position you are offering me, and I will be glad to take it. I just wish someone would come and offer that man in there a job for thirty shillings a week. It would give him a reason for living.'

The two young women stood silent for a moment, the other's sad acceptance somehow depressing.

'When . . . when can you start?' Mona inquired, after a moment.

'You will be knowing I lost my

position with Willie Young, so I am able to start right away,' Mrs McNeill answered in the quaint phrasing of the Gael speaking English.

Flora went cold. 'When . . . how . . . what happened?'

'He heard of me saying there was no engagement and would be no marriage between you and him.' Mrs McNeill sighed. 'He handed me my books, and wouldn't pay me for my day's wages because I had 'defamed his character'. The man is gone mad!' she ended with calm certainty.

'Indeed, yes, quite mad!' Mona agreed breezily. 'But it couldn't have happened at a better time for me. The flat desperately needs help. And maybe once you've started you could tell me what needs to be done to it.'

A little later, on top of a tram going to Shawlands, Mona suddenly broke the silence which had settled on them when they left Govan.

'Just think, I'll need to get up at six in the morning!'

A faint smile broke the seriousness of Flora's face. Mrs McNeill was to come at seven next morning to allow Mona to see her, before she herself went out to work. Flora wished that getting up early was her main worry. From what Mrs McNeill had said, Willie Young was still convinced that she would marry him.

The thought filled her with horror. She desperately hoped her brother, Robert, would go to see him and force him into giving up these notions.

'Why did she keep us outside the door?' Mona asked suddenly.

'Maybe her husband was in bed,' Flora answered practically. 'The middle houses there are single-ends — just one room.'

'You mean that big lad, Roddy, the little girl and the parents share it?' Mona was amazed.

'Could be a few more children living there, too,' Flora wryly assured her.

That evening Aunt Isa was eager to hear Flora's news about her meeting with Hamish and the visit to Govan to offer Mrs McNeill the job of looking after the flat next door.

Flora could not bring herself to speak to her aunt about Willie Young's reasons for sacking Mrs McNeill — that he still maintained he was engaged to be married to her. She knew it was perhaps weak of her, but she yearned with all her heart for the whole thing to disappear.

Suddenly, Aunt Isa stopped talking and sat listening for a few moments.

'They're at it again!' She sighed. The sound of angry voices on the landing filtered through to them in the comfortable living-room. Two sharp bursts of the doorbell broke the silence and they knew their neighbours were at the door. Moments later the angry little figure of Mrs McLaurin came into the room.

★　★　★

'Not a word was said to me that a woman was coming to work in my house, with my furniture!' she said.

'After all, Mr Alexander put *my* name on the rent book, and I should have at least been consulted.'

'Loly, I couldn't tell you — I was in bed when you came home. And you were still asleep when I left this morning.' Mona followed in after her. 'Anyway, we'd agreed that I would need help — so what's the big worry because I've got someone?'

'But I was arranging that — I told you I'd see to it!' Mrs McLaurin said huffily. 'Disgraceful conduct, not even being consulted. I'd said I would stay on until we got something fixed, and what happens — I am ignored and things are settled over my head!'

Isa Rennie and her niece were becoming used to the wrangling between her neighbours, and their growing habit of bringing the disagreements across the landing. Isa now realised she was expected to arbitrate.

'I would be quite within my rights if I told this person to go away and not dare enter the house!' Mrs McLaurin announced.

'Loly, if you upset Mrs McNeill, I'll never forgive you!' Mona stared belligerently at the little woman who had been part of her life since she was a child.

'Now, now!' Isa was soothing. 'We must understand each other's point of view.' And as usual she managed to sympathise with Mrs McLaurin's hurt at not being consulted, and Mona's desire to get help quickly now that Mrs McLaurin was going back to help with Nadia's coming baby.

As they all ate a little supper later, an uneasy peace, more akin to a truce, held between the little woman and the scowling Mona. It was a relief when they left, for resentment still simmered.

Next morning Mrs McLaurin packed all her clothes and went back to live in her old rooms in the Pollokshields mansion. Privately, Isa Rennie thought if Mona had only offered a few reconciling words, the little woman would not have moved out completely. But Mona remained stiffly unbending.

As a week went by, the comfort of having Mrs McNeill cleaning the flat and leaving a meal prepared, and a warm fire to greet her return in the evening, confirmed to Mona that she was in the right.

A puzzled Bartie approached Mona and Flora at their morning tea-break.

'What's happening? I've to take all that furniture I took to your flat back to the Pollokshields house.'

Mona stared at him in disbelief. 'That's vindictive! Loly's leaving me without a bed to sleep in.' She shook her head. 'She's trying to get the upper hand. Thinks without furniture I'll be forced to return to the old house — but I won't!'

'That's old stuff!' Bartie grinned. 'For a tenner you could replace it and better.'

'How? Where?' Mona asked eagerly.

'I know a man,' Bartie said complacently. 'Tell him what you want and

146

your price and he'll get it for you.'

Flora watched them uneasily as they planned to meet the man that evening. Mona had been subdued all week since Mrs McLaurin moved out, but now she was in high spirits, as if thwarting the older woman's plans gave her life a new impetus.

★　★　★

In the shop there was an air of suppressed excitement and expectancy. Rumours were going round of staff promotions. Mr Lambie had decided to train an assistant for the wines and spirits department. Tom, Dick and Harry on the ham counter were especially interested.

'Don't suppose I've got a chance,' Tom Miller said despondently to Flora. He was the top ham boner and was always Mr Lambie's choice for it.

Near closing time on the Wednesday evening, everyone watched with interest as Isa went and informed Tom that Mr

Hugh wanted to speak to him. Then she went to the back shop and told Jamie Morton to wait behind.

Jamie looked near to tears at the news. He thought his pranks on Roderick McNeill had not been forgotten after all.

As she left the shop, Flora was surprised to see the tall figure of Hamish Buchanan waiting outside for her.

'I knew I would catch you now.' He smiled. 'All going well, the papers finalising the sale of your father's books will be ready for signing at the weekend. I've just written to your brothers, suggesting they be signed on Saturday,' he said. 'Also, the American buyer has offered to pay all legal fees and the agent's commission if it's settled by this weekend.'

'That's wonderful! It was very kind of you to come and tell me personally,' Flora murmured, although her heart was sore that her father's books would now definitely go to a stranger. He'd looked on each of them as a close friend.

Hamish saw the look on her face and rushed to reassure her. 'This American is actually a Scot by extraction and he's eager that the collection be kept together. I think he'll cherish them.'

Flora smiled up at him, grateful for his sensitivity.

Then her smile froze. Willie Young was standing on the other side of the road, scowling over at her.

Hamish noticed the change in her immediately, and put his hand out to steady her as she seemed to sway.

'Willie Young . . . he's across there . . . watching . . . '

'Come on — let's get you into Bartie's car,' Hamish said urgently. He put a protective arm about her and drew her over to the car at the kerb.

Mona was already sitting in the front.

'Come with us, Hamish!' she sang out when she saw him. 'We're going to choose furniture for my flat.'

'Why not! It'll be a new experience.'

Hamish did not hesitate and, after helping Flora into the back, got in beside her.

Soon the four of them were in a shop down a back street off the Saltmarket. It was packed from floor to ceiling with all types of second-hand furniture, some of it almost new.

Bartie wrangled with Sandy, the dealer, over the different pieces, and good-naturedly refused some of them as being too well used.

'Tell you what — I was at a Warrant Sale today and got some first-class furniture.' Sandy turned to Mona.

'If you can up your amount, my dear, I'll let you have it. See? It's still in my van.' He led them out to a van parked outside.

Flora hung back. She hated anything to do with Warrant Sales. She remembered when one of their long-standing neighbours got into arrears with the rent and rates. She'd seen their humiliation when Sheriff's Officers came and broke their door down.

They'd almost cleared the house of furniture and dumped it on the pavement outside, where dealers like Sandy came and bought it for a pittance to clear the debt.

Hamish nodded when she tried to explain. 'Yes, it's a cruel way to get debt cleared.'

But Mona was delighted when she came back in. 'I'm taking the lot! And I've made a deal — the sable coat!'

'Wasn't that a bit impetuous?' Hamish queried.

'Probably!' Mona shrugged. 'But I've completely furnished the flat down to pots, pans, crockery, cutlery, drawers full of bed linen and blankets . . . in exchange for a coat I don't wear. I'd never have thought of using it if your Aunt Isa hadn't told me I could when I was short of ready cash!' Mona told Flora.

She was in a state of high excitement, anxious that the furniture be taken immediately to the flat.

'We can't move all the furniture in

tonight,' Bartie declared. 'Sandy's men have gone home, so there's nobody at the other end to help me carry it upstairs.'

'Oh, no! I want it right away,' Mona said petulantly. She turned eagerly to Hamish. 'You could borrow one of Bartie's brown overalls and help him take the stuff up.'

'Are you so desperate?' Hamish chuckled.

Mona nodded vigorously. 'It would only take ten minutes.'

'All right, all right!' Hamish laughed as Mona threw her arms round his neck, and kissed him full on the lips.

Sandy drove his van to the Shawlands flat with an excited Mona beside him to direct. Bartie stopped off at his small yard and picked up his van while Hamish took over the wheel of the car and drove Flora back to Shawlands.

When they got there Flora took a quick look round, almost afraid that Willie Young might have taken up loitering there, too. Being with Hamish did give her a sense of security, but she dreaded meeting Willie on her own.

The sable coat was handed over to the dealer, and Hamish and Bartie carried the furniture upstairs, then on the return journey brought Mrs McLaurin's down to Bartie's van. In just over an hour the switch had been made.

Flora was intrigued to see Mona engrossed, contemplating the best position for her new possessions. In a very short time the flat was transformed.

Aunt Isa returned from the shop after the interviews just as the final pieces were being placed. She was very impressed with Mona's purchases, but Flora saw the look of dismay on her face when she learned the furniture was from a Warrant Sale.

She had brought a large steak pie from the butcher and some fancy cakes from the kiosk and invited them all in for supper.

Flora enjoyed these impromptu meals and the bustle and laughter as everyone helped with the preparations and setting the table.

At the door, before Hamish took his leave, he suggested to Flora that she could sign the papers after work on Friday.

'It will save you from having to ask for time off,' Hamish explained. 'Come straight from the shop and meet me at the Newark Hotel, facing Queen's Park. Then after the signing we'll have a little supper to round things off.'

Flora was happy to agree. It was the first time she'd been invited out on her own by a young man. She didn't count the time when she had filled in at the last minute as Ralph Anderson's partner at the student end-of-term dance. The fussy, pink evening dress she'd borrowed from her sister-in-law hadn't quite fitted, and she'd felt shy and awkward.

★　★　★

Next day there was a feeling of extra energy in the shop as the promotions came into force. Tom Miller exchanged the large apron of the ham counter for the white coat overall of the wines and spirits. A large new rubber apron would now be kept in the basement for him, to use when he was bottling Lambies' own special blend of whisky, a local favourite.

Jamie Morton's eyes shone as he put on the big, wrap-round apron and hung the large knife sharpener by his side like a sword. Even Aunt Isa's long talk on the do's and don'ts could not quench his enthusiasm. Being on Lambies' ham counter meant he was now a person of some worth.

Dick and Harry were disappointed that they were not chosen for the more prestigious job on the wines and spirits counter, but they had moved up half a notch, in that Harry now took over Tom's old duties and Dick took over Harry's.

Mona was only vaguely interested when Flora told her about meeting Hamish on Friday to sign the papers and have supper. She was suddenly immersed in the improvements to the flat, arranging for Mr McNeill, Catriona's husband, to come and do some decorating.

'Catriona says he does it all in their flat, despite only having one arm. And young Roddy will come and help with the heavy stuff after his work,' Mona explained at lunchtime on Friday, when she came in laden with pots of paints and rolls of paper.

Privately, Flora wondered how a one-armed man could possibly hang wallpaper. But as Mona was so excited about it she didn't want to dampen her enthusiasm. Besides, she was a little preoccupied herself thinking about her meeting with Hamish.

At closing time she hurried along Victoria Road towards Queen's Park, the pavements still busy with late-night shoppers. Despite herself, she kept taking quick glances about her, afraid that Willie Young might still be spying on her.

It was a relief to come to the steps of the hotel and see Hamish waiting at the door. Inside, the hotel was comfortably unpretentious.

The signing of the papers only took seconds, and then they sat in the quiet restaurant at a small corner table and chatted informally.

Hamish spoke admiringly of his cousin Bartie's new car.

'Maybe in a year or so I'll be able to afford one,' he said. 'Or sooner, if our senior partner retires — he'll be eighty next birthday.' He laughed ruefully. 'Old Mr McMorrin won't allow any of his deeds or dispositions to be typed in the modern way — they've still got to be hand-written for him.'

Hamish described how in the old days the apprentices often got this job, but Hodges, their clerk, wrote them now for his old master.

'Can't help wishing he'd hurry up and retire. I'll not get promoted up the partners' ladder until he does,'

Hamish admitted. 'And Hodges gets fed up writing out the deeds. It's time-consuming and he's got other duties.'

Flora was fascinated, listening to his stories about the lawyer's office and how it functioned. Then she reminisced about her parents, and told him of Aunt Isa's disapproval of her father and his love of knowledge and the money he spent on books.

'Your father's hobby has certainly paid off now.' Hamish smiled.

'Do you remember your father? Did he have a hobby?' she asked.

'No, my father . . . He's spent a lot of his life in hospital. He got shell-shocked in the war and his memory comes and goes. Often he doesn't know me, and lately doesn't recognise my mother.'

Flora coloured. She'd been sure his mother was a widow.

'I'm sorry — I didn't realise,' she apologised.

'It's all right!' He shrugged, then

smiled wryly. 'Yet, maybe you'll understand it's made my mother how she is. She's had to be strong, and make the decisions.'

Flora nodded, strangely touched that he should defend and explain his mother's abrasive manner.

And his was a familiar story, few families in the country hadn't suffered because of the war.

★ ★ ★

For the next couple of weeks, Mona's regard for the McNeills grew daily. And Aunt Isa and Flora were impressed by the improvement in her flat as, gradually, each room was transformed with fresh paint and paper.

'I'd never have believed a one-armed man could have tackled this,' Aunt Isa murmured as Mona showed them the transformation.

'Catriona helps him, and so does young Roddy,' Mona answered. 'But I wish he could get a real job. He's so intelligent. In fact, I've decided to ask Bartie. He's thinking of expanding his business. I'm sure Donald John would be an asset.'

Next day, when Bartie was delivering to the shop, Mona waylaid him and after extolling Donald John's virtues asked Bartie to employ him.

'He could work the office for you for just thirty shillings a week!' Mona enthused.

'For ten shillings a week a wee lassie out of school could do all my office work just now,' Bartie said tolerantly. 'Anyway, when I take on a man he'll need to be able to drive and work alongside me.'

'Yes, but I'm sure you could use him,' Mona pleaded.

'No.' Bartie shook his head. 'If I could, I would. But my business can't afford to pay a man's wages just now.'

'But — but . . . I've told him I would get him fixed up.' Mona said almost accusingly. 'You've said business was doing well.'

'Yes, and I'm working towards employing another man in time. But he'll have to have two arms and a strong back like myself!' Bartie said firmly.

Tears of disappointment filled Mona's eyes as she stopped at the kiosk.

'What am I going to say to Catriona and Donald John? They think I'll be able to get him a job with Bartie, but he won't even consider it.'

Flora did not know how to answer, for Bartie's caution was understandable. His business had just started to give some return. And she realised Mona's generous impulses had over-reached her capabilities.

'My bathroom needs painting. Tell Donald John he can start doing it on Monday,' Aunt Isa said suddenly.

'Yes.' Mona nodded, but she was more subdued. Donald John really needed lighter work. She'd noticed after two weeks decorating in the flat he was looking very drawn and tired.

Mona left to go back to the office and Aunt Isa sighed.

'She'll have to realise that because she desperately wants to help, it doesn't happen as a matter of course.'

No Witnesses

Being Friday, Flora met Mona for the snack break in the late afternoon. Now Mona was more than somewhat disgruntled with Bartie. And Flora knew she thought he was being less than generous.

'He could have helped Donald John,' she said sulkily, watching Bartie as he carried boxes into the back store.

'Be practical!' Flora said sharply. 'Carriers need two arms.'

'He just didn't want to help!' Mona persisted, ignoring Flora's logic.

Flora was about to retaliate, but she stopped. She knew Mona loathed being thwarted so words were wasted at the moment. Just then Mr Hugh, followed by Ralph Anderson, came into the back shop and made for the staff table. Both girls immediately thought of Nadia, Mona's stepmother, as Ralph was attending her.

Flora got up, ready to leave quietly. But Mr Hugh raised a restraining hand. 'This young man would like a quick word with you,' he said jovially.

'Right, Doctor — there's still five minutes of the snack break left.'

'I'm grateful,' Ralph Anderson murmured.

Flora was surprised that he looked embarrassed, as he scrabbled in an inside jacket pocket, and brought out large, gilt-edged tickets.

'My two senior colleagues were taking their wives to this medical ball tonight.' He laid the tickets on the table and looked appealingly at Flora. 'They can't go, but someone has to represent the practice and they've asked me . . . '

Mona swooped on the tickets. 'There's four — that's Flora and I and you and . . . Have you another man in mind?' Her eyes danced and she gazed provocatively up at him.

Flora watched in dismay. Surely Mona wasn't flirting with him? What was she up to?

'No . . . actually . . . since it's such short notice I was just thinking . . . ' Ralph started looking towards Flora again.

'Tell you what.' Mona jumped up and linked her arm in his. 'I'll partner you and Flora can get Bartie!' She called over, 'Bartie, get into your dinner-suit, and be at the Central Hotel for eight tonight!'

Bartie looked up, smiling as usual. 'No!' he replied briefly.

Mona went home an hour early that Friday evening, and packed two evening dresses. She hurried to the Central Hotel and met Flora with Hamish Buchanan just before eight o'clock. He had agreed to take Bartie's place to make up the four.

The two girls changed in the powder room at high speed, and managed to reach their seats just as the top table were being piped in. Flora had no time to feel nervous. All the people she was introduced to then were just a haze of faces. Yet, as the evening went on, she discovered they were mostly young doctors with whom Ralph had studied. Like her they had never learned the modern dances, but remembered the Scottish country dances from their school days.

As soon as one was announced Flora was swept on to the floor and had to keep up with the enthusiasm and high spirits of her partners. She loved it. After a strenuous Eightsome Reel her partner led her back to her table. As they approached she noticed Ralph was sitting staring into the middle distance, a worried look on his face.

As soon as he became aware of them, he put on a cheerful smile.

Flora sat down breathlessly. The figure-hugging red dress with a small kick train at the back she was wearing was not really suitable for a reel, but some of Ralph's medical colleagues had insisted she make up their eight, threatening to lift her bodily on to the floor if she refused!

'I never realised how wholeheartedly

medical men throw themselves into their play!' Flora gasped.

'You've been quite the belle of the ball tonight.' Ralph smiled from the seat opposite.

'Having a generous friend who lends from her extensive wardrobe helps.' Flora smoothed the borrowed dress which fitted as if made for her. She sensed his preoccupation, despite his attempts to keep up a conversation.

'Do you ever hear from Kirsty?' she asked quietly.

He looked at her, startled, then gave a little laugh. 'Ah, yes, I remember as a student confiding in you my hopeless regard for her.' He smiled a little sheepishly. 'Actually, Kirsty returns my feelings now.'

'I couldn't be more pleased!' Then Flora looked at him, puzzled. 'You don't seem as happy about it as I thought you would.'

'I'm over the moon, but how can I ask her to marry me?' He sighed deeply. 'I've had an offer to buy into a practice, but I need two thousand pounds and I haven't got that many pennies towards a deposit. And the bank needs some sort of guarantee . . . ' He shrugged and shook his head at the impossibility of the situation.

Just then, Hamish and Mona came back to the table from dancing. Mona was in high spirits and she grabbed Ralph. 'Next dance is a foxtrot and it's time you learned it!' As the dance band stuck up Mona pulled a mildly-protesting Ralph to the floor. Like the other young doctors, he never had time to learn the modern dances.

* * *

'Don't know where she gets her energy from,' Hamish murmured, mopping his brow and trying to ease the stiff collar round his neck. 'She's either on a high, or feeling desperately low.' He leaned forward. 'What happened tonight with Bartie? She seems quite peeved with him.'

168

Flora paused to choose her words. She couldn't tell him about Mona flirting with Ralph in front of Bartie.

'He did have a job booked for tonight — and . . . well, she didn't so much ask as order Bartie to attend. And there was also the business of Bartie refusing to employ her daily woman's husband.'

Hamish smiled and nodded knowingly as Flora sketched in the background.

'I can understand her wanting to get Donald John work,' Flora finished. 'He's highly intelligent, even taught himself to write copper-plate with his left hand.'

'That's interesting!' Hamish suddenly became serious. 'Do you think he'd be able to write out deeds?'

'His writing would certainly grace any legal document,' Flora answered.

'We could give him a few hours a week on old Mr McMorrin's work,' Hamish mused. 'In fact, if he could cope, he'd get a full week of it.'

When Mona came back to the table and heard Hamish's suggestion she was jubilant, assuring him that Donald John was exactly what he needed.

'Oh, hold on! We'd need to see him first, before we could offer anything.'

'Donald John's your man!' Mona was happily confident. 'This has made my day, together with Ralph's news just now that my little sister or brother will probably appear next month, and Nadia is positively blooming!'

'And as I also said,' Ralph put in pointedly, 'Nadia would love a visit from you *before* then.'

'Yes . . . yes . . . Flora and I will go on Sunday,' Mona agreed airily, taking Flora's consent for granted.

Flora nodded her agreement. Mona had avoided going to visit her old home, especially since the coolness between herself and Mrs McLaurin, the housekeeper. Flora hoped they would make up for Mona was miserable about it. She was hiding it behind all sorts of activity.

After midnight, tea and biscuits were served, and Flora began to feel tired, especially thinking that she had to be at Lambies' for eight next morning. She suggested going home.

'Oh, no! The night is young!' Mona declaimed in mock acting style.

'I'll take Flora home. It's a bit late for me, too,' Ralph offered.

Twenty minutes later his car drew up at her close.

'By the way, did I jump in too quickly just now, offering to drive you home?' he asked as Flora got in. 'Thought the young lawyer looked a bit put out.'

'Oh, no.' Flora smiled. 'Hamish and Mona are friends.'

'Thanks for coming. You got me out of a difficult situation.' He smiled. 'These occasions are important for a practice like ours, whose patients come from private and panel.'

'Why didn't you ask Kirsty to go?'

'It's her parents' Silver Wedding tonight. I'd been invited,' Ralph murmured ruefully.

'Shame! Hope things work out for you both.' Flora smiled, and got out of the car. With a wave she walked into the close as he drove off.

★　★　★

Flora was still smiling as she climbed the stairs, remembering how Ralph used to talk incessantly about Kirsty in his student days. All his life he'd worshipped her from afar; the only daughter of the big farm neighbouring his father's small dairy spread in Ayrshire. Flora wondered how they had finally managed to get together . . .

She had almost reached the top landing when she froze. Willie Young stood there, barring her way. Flora bit her lip to prevent herself from screaming.

'I've been waiting to get an answer from you personally about my proposal,' he said truculently, his voice slurred.

She spoke in a quiet, controlled voice. 'I will be quite brutal. I have no wish to marry you!'

'Why not? You could live in the lap of luxury, married to me. There's few who know how well off I am!'

'Mr Young!' Flora persisted. 'Weeks ago my brother, Robert, specially visited you to tell you that I didn't wish to accept your proposal — he also asked you to stop saying publicly that there was an engagement between us.'

Willie Young stared at her and his lip curled in derision. He took a step forward and she realised he had been drinking. She backed away but he caught the lapels of her coat, and shook her.

'You'll marry me . . . ' he snarled.

'No, I won't!' Flora managed as her head was jerked back and forward. She twisted, pulling away from him. When he released her suddenly, she staggered and fell. There was blinding pain as her face hit the tiled wall. As she lay on the steps feeling dazed and sick, she became aware of blood trickling from her mouth and nose.

For a moment Willie stood motionless, his face registering horror at what he had done. Then his eyes darted furtively about. 'Don't try to charge me. There's no witnesses!' he rasped, then turned and charged downstairs as the door behind him began to open.

'Flora, what on earth . . . '

'That was Willie Young . . . ' Flora croaked, tears welling up as her face started to throb. 'Go in, Aunt Isa, you'll get cold.'

Isa Rennie disappeared inside and Flora picked up her handbag and slowly walked up the last few stairs to the open front door.

'Blood is getting on to your dress. Quick, get it off so that it won't stain!' Aunt Isa shrieked, and in moments, Flora was propelled into the small kitchenette where Aunt Isa whisked off the dress and put it into a solution of cold water and salt.

In just half an hour Flora began to feel more normal. The cold compresses Aunt Isa had held to her face took the sting of pain away and stopped the swelling.

'I must look a sight!' Flora tried to laugh a little as her fingertips explored the tender places on her face.

'You'll have a black eye in the morning.' Aunt Isa sniffed, reapplying the cold, newly-wrung-out flannel. 'That man has got to be stopped — once and for all! I am not a woman who believes in violence but there comes a time when you have to defend yourself. I will speak to Bartie Darroch.'

'Bartie?' Flora was puzzled. She'd thought her aunt might mention Hamish. 'Wouldn't it be better if Hamish sent him a lawyer's letter?'

'No! Willie Young is a bully. I remember him from the playground when we were children,' Aunt Isa fumed. 'And bullies are cowards, afraid of suffering the pain they inflict on others. A little rough handling will do more good than any lawyer's letter, and Bartie Darroch is just the one to administer it.'

'But we . . . I . . . can't involve Bartie. It's nothing to do with him!' Flora protested.

'I think Bartie would like to be involved, especially where you are concerned,' Aunt Isa declared.

'Oh, no . . . ' Flora wailed softly as a fresh rush of tears threatened to overwhelm her again.

The doorbell rang twice just then. Aunt Isa went to open the door.

'The dance went dead after Flora and Ralph left . . . ' Mona's voice floated through to Flora. 'Hamish and I saw your lights on . . . ' She came into the living-room followed by Hamish, then gasped when she saw Flora sitting holding the cold compress to her face.

'That evil man Willie Young was waiting for her,' Aunt Isa announced grimly. 'He attacked her!'

'Have you told the police?' Mona asked.

'Oh, no . . . no!' Flora almost shrieked. 'They can't do anything — there were no witnesses — and Willie

Young knows it.'

'We must do something! He can't be allowed to act like that!' Mona was appalled. 'Hamish, isn't there anything in law that can be done?'

Hamish shook his head. 'Nothing that would deter that man. A lawyer's letter could be sent, but he's a crafty type who knows all the tricks.'

'That's why I am going to approach your cousin, Bartie. I think perhaps if he . . . spoke to him firmly, that might have some effect.' Aunt Isa's primly-chosen words had an emphasis which left them in no doubt of her true intention.

'Yes,' Hamish's frown changed to a smile of assent. 'I couldn't have put it better myself. Bartie is just the man for the job!'

* * *

In bed later Flora slept fitfully, wakening again and again as the nightmare of Willie Young's face, inches from her own, was relived in her dreams. She was glad when morning came, and Aunt Isa came through to her with a cup of tea.

'I've put plenty of milk in it to cool it down for your poor mouth,' Aunt Isa fussed. 'And I'm afraid you can't go to business today. Not looking like that.'

'Oh dear, what will Mr Lambie think?' Flora sighed.

'He, and everyone else in the shop, knows about Willie Young's antics. He will understand your predicament. Just stay in your bed and rest.' Aunt Isa brooked no argument.

Flora was grateful to her aunt, but this last incident made her painfully aware of the loss of her parents. When they were alive, she took for granted the feeling of loving security they gave. But now she felt vulnerable, and very alone.

Then once again Mona's shrill double ring of the front doorbell jerked her out of the despondency. A radiant Mona rushed into her bedroom, brandishing a picture postcard.

'It's from my father — he's in Paris!' Tears of delight shone in Mona's eyes. She buried her face in her hands and sobbed for a few moments, then sniffed and scrubbed her eyes with her handkerchief.

'Stupid to cry when I'm so happy!'

That morning Aunt Isa and Mona travelled to work in silence, both occupied with their separate thoughts.

Mona had to keep swallowing to control the emotions which kept welling up within her. By turns she was elated and wanted to sing and shout for joy that her father had contacted her — that he was well, and thinking about her. Then she felt like weeping her heart out with the relief of it.

Isa's lips were folded in a prim line to contain her fury that Willie Young had dared to lay hands on her niece. When, at first Flora came to stay with her, Isa had looked on it as a necessary duty. But in the months since she had developed a deep affection for the girl.

As soon as she got into the shop she

went to find Hugh Lambie. He was in the little office above the wines and spirits counter. But his brother Rab was with him. Isa was put out, for Rab, the oldest of the Lambie brothers, ran the Byres Road branch and was accepted as the senior in the business. He had a curt, almost rough manner, and did not hold Aunt Isa in as much respect as his brother.

Hugh would never over-ride any of Isa's wishes about the running of the Crosshill branch, but his brother Rab had no such reserve.

'Ah, Isa, just the person I want to see,' Rab started immediately. 'That cake, coffee and confectionery counter of yours is running well, and I hear your assistant is fully trained.'

'My niece, Flora, has been an excellent choice,' Aunt Isa answered.

'Good. Well, I want one of you to come and start the same thing in the Byres Road shop. There'll be a good raise in wages for both of you whatever you decide.'

Aunt Isa stiffened. Rab Lambie's directness was a little too blunt for her taste. And she never thought of herself earning a wage, but a salary.

'It will have to be myself, then,' Aunt Isa announced, and went on in a brittle voice. 'My niece is being persecuted and pursued by a man who has business interests in the West End. Last night he waylaid her just after midnight coming from the Medical Ball in the Central Hotel. He was waiting on the landing, and attacked her when she refused to marry him . . . '

Aunt Isa almost enjoyed the growing concern and disbelief on the faces of the two men, especially Rab Lambie's.

'Willie Young!' Rab cried. 'So it's your niece he's making a fool of himself over. Becoming a real laughing stock.'

'Maybe so — but Flora is a quiet, cultured sort of girl — far beyond his class. She's lying at home with her face cut and bruised, in a state of shock and worry because she couldn't come to business this morning.'

'Just you leave him to me!' Rab Lambie was decisive, his heavy black eyebrows meeting in a fierce frown. 'I'll put his gas at a peep. He's not going to harm any of my employees. Tell the girl to rest easy, he'll not bother her again after I've seen him.'

Aunt Isa was taken off balance. She had not thought that Rab Lambie would react like this — but then, she hadn't known he would be here.

The whole matter being taken so abruptly and unexpectedly from her disconcerted Aunt Isa. But, Rab Lambie *was* the ideal person to deal with the situation — and she knew it. Yet as she came down the wooden steps from the office she felt disgruntled and put out.

Bartie was waiting for her, looking concerned. 'Hamish phoned me early this morning about Flora. He suggested we both go to see this Willie Young and . . . '

'No, no, Bartie!' Aunt Isa held up a hand delicately. 'Rab Lambie is here this morning and he has taken it on himself to do just that.' Aunt Isa paused and quelled any stirrings of resentment, and her innate honesty took over. 'Rab Lambie knows Willie Young — we were all at school together. And as Flora is his employee, he sees it as a duty to protect her.'

'I don't think Hamish had slept. He'd got on to me first thing — raging over Flora's injuries,' Bartie said.

'Very thoughtful!' Aunt Isa murmured, and hurried to her counter.

Mona ran up to Bartie, holding her postcard aloft.

'From my father!' she said excitedly. 'He's safe and well!'

'That's a big weight of sorrow taken from you,' Bartie murmured, patting her shoulder. 'I'm glad for you.'

They stood talking for a few more minutes, while Mona poured out all her relief, last night's annoyance with him forgotten.

'Must dash!' She giggled. 'The big boss is in today, and he's sent me to take Flora's place in the cake kiosk. Wish me luck, for I'm under a hard taskmaster in Aunt Isa.'

Bartie turned back to unloading his van, a smile on his face. When Mona was happy the whole world seemed a brighter place.

Meanwhile, in Isa's Shawlands' flat, Flora lay in bed dozing. The key turned in the door and a tall, well-dressed woman came into the bedroom holding a piece of paper. Flora blinked and stared uncomprehendingly until Catriona McNeill spoke.

'Flora Lochart, I'm hearing that madman has visited you again. And what a mess he has made of you.' She quickly appraised Flora's injuries. 'I hope you will soon be well,' she said formally, before she rushed on, indicating the paper. 'Miss Alexander says here there may be work for Donald John with a lawyer — and you could give me the details.'

It took Flora a moment to marshal her thoughts, and think back to

Hamish's suggestions last night. It all seemed so long ago. But she told Catriona all he had said.

'Donald John will need a suit.' Catriona frowned and looked down at the finely-tailored coat she was wearing. 'I went to that man your aunt sent me to for Roderick's working clothes. Donald John insisted I get clothes out of the money he earned for the decorating of Miss Alexander's place — but it's a suit he should have got!'

'Don't build up your hopes. Maybe Donald John won't be — ' Flora stopped, searching for the right word, for she could see Catriona already bristling at what she thought was a coming slur on her husband's capabilities.

' . . . There's many a slip twixt the cup and the lip, as my mother used to say,' Flora finished a little lamely.

Flora hoped Hamish would be able to use her husband in the office.

Hamish was a gentleman in every sense of the word. And while she lay half asleep, thoughts of Hamish flitted in and out of her dreams . . .

★ ★ ★

It was a shock when she opened her eyes and found him standing by her bed. Her first thought was how awful she must look, her hair hadn't been combed yet this morning.

'Mr Buchanan has come to see you,' Catriona announced behind him, her face now softened with a happy smile. 'I'll just be bringing you both a cup of coffee — Miss Alexander would expect it of me,' she said as she left them alone.

'Just fixed up an interview for the famous Donald John for Monday morning,' Hamish said, pulling over a chair and sitting astride it, his arms resting on the back. He smiled and leaned closer to examine her face. 'Your injuries add a bit of interest to your attractions.'

'Doesn't feel too bad now,' Flora

offered, touching her lips with her fingertips. 'I'm scared to look.'

'You're just as lovely as ever!' Hamish said gallantly. 'And I'm here to tell you it won't happen again.' He told her how Rab Lambie was going to force the issue with Willie Young.

Flora listened and hoped with all her heart it was true, for now she was truly terrified of Willie Young. She couldn't cope with him. He was, indeed, a madman!

'Got a call from Bartie — he and Mona are friends again. Last night's friction forgotten.' He grinned. 'And she's heard from her father, too, did you know?'

Flora nodded and told him about the postcard. She'd thought he would be delighted but his calm acceptance of the news puzzled her. Hamish seemed more interested then in talking about the theatre scene in Glasgow.

A Bluff Kindliness

Did you go to the Royal for any of the Brandon-Thomas season in the autumn?' Hamish Buchanan asked.

She shook her head. 'My father was very ill, then.'

'Ah, yes — you must make a point then of seeing this season's plays — there's Barrie's 'Quality Street', John Drinkwater's 'Bird In Hand', John Van Druten's 'London Wall' . . . '

'Actually, I've never been to the theatre,' Flora interrupted quickly, for he was ready to discuss the repertory company of which she had no knowledge.

'Never? That's extraordinary, as you're so well read.'

'My father found books all absorbing, and couldn't afford the theatre as a hobby, too,' she murmured.

'We'll have to remedy that!' Hamish

exclaimed. 'I'll book a couple of seats for each of us for the plays in the coming weeks. Would you like that?'

'Oh, well, yes! I've always wanted to go to the Rep,' Flora replied, puzzled that he should invite her while not mentioning Mona.

'You won't have attended any of the Carl Rosa Opera Company's performances, either. They're doing their 1935 two-week season in the King's.' Hamish was almost boyish in his eagerness, detailing the coming operas; 'Die Fledermaus', 'Don Giovanni', 'Faust', 'Carmen', 'Rigoletto', and the rest he thought they might attend.

'You'll love it! And I'll enjoy introducing you to a whole new world!' he said enthusiastically.

Just then Catriona came in with their coffee tray. 'I met a couple just now who say they are your brother and sister-in-law. They're very insistent that they be allowed to see you, Flora — especially the woman.'

Flora knew immediately from Catriona's frosty tone that it must be Milly and Robert. Milly had that effect on people. Moments later the tall, stooped figure of Robert came in followed by his wife.

'Who is that woman?' Milly began, but her husband silenced her with a look.

'We've just heard about your attack, Flora,' Robert said anxiously. 'Rab Lambie came to see me at the bank — what on earth happened? Willie Young's in hospital. The staff found him in the back shop first thing this morning — unconscious!'

Flora felt the blood drain from her face, as she stared in horror at her brother and his wife, standing by her bed.

'Willie Young — unconscious!' she whispered.

'Here, steady on — don't faint!' Hamish Buchanan reached over and took her hand, rubbing it between his palms.

Flora felt the colour rush back, very aware of Hamish's touch.

'I'm all right!' She gave a nervous laugh, then explained to Robert and Milly about last night's incident with the drunken Willie Young — all the while conscious that Hamish had not released her hand.

'Is there any more news from the hospital?' she asked her brother.

Robert shrugged. 'I don't know. When Rab Lambie went to the shop he saw Willie Young's sister — the one who works there during the day. She said Willie was in hospital.'

Flora listened with strained interest. Cissie Young was a capable, officious, person. Indeed, she was the mainstay of the business.

That Rab Lambie had involved himself with her troubles amazed Flora. She had never met the man, although he was one of her employers. He seldom came to the Crosshill branch, and Aunt Isa seemed to disapprove of him, somehow.

'Why did Willie Young go back to the shop so late at night instead of going home?' Hamish queried slowly. 'An easier place to finish off his drinking session, perhaps?'

The other three looked at him blankly, puzzled at his unexpected question.

'As a matter of fact,' Robert turned towards him. 'Rab Lambie did mention the back shop smelled like a brewery, and Cissie Young was furious. She's been a lifelong member of the Band of Hope.'

'I suggest, then,' Hamish declared, 'that Willie, when the staff found him this morning, wasn't so much unconscious as blind drunk. But seeing the blood on him from his fall on the stairs here last night, they jumped to the wrong conclusion. No doubt his sister knew better and thought waking up in a hospital bed might sober him up!'

'The legal mind at work?' Milly giggled.

'Having met the man,' Robert

remarked, 'that's probably nearer the truth than any of us have yet considered.'

The horror which had enveloped Flora since Willie Young's attack started to recede. Hamish's interpretation seemed to reduce the enormity of the incident in her mind, and she was grateful to him.

Soon after, Hamish got up to leave, reminding her that he would get theatre tickets and to keep her Tuesdays free.

It was a relief when Milly and Robert left and Flora was glad to lie back against her pillows and close her eyes. She felt relaxed now, since Hamish's visit, and she soon drifted off to sleep.

She could hardly believe two hours had elapsed when the door opened again and Aunt Isa bustled in followed by a tall, middle-aged man. Flora recognised him at once as Rab Lambie. His likeness to his brother Hugh was apparent, although he was a slightly rougher, untidier version.

'Rab Lambie, at your service!' he

boomed, taking her hand. 'And don't try to sit up — I've just come to assure you that Willie Young won't be troubling you again.'

He sat down in the chair Hamish had vacated and, in a few short sentences, told her that Willie Young was being sent to live in his mother's house in Carmunnock.

His sister and her husband-to-be were taking over the business, and Willie would be paid a wage to stay away.

'I'm very grateful,' Flora murmured. 'Why he got such a fixation to marry me, I don't know. Maybe it was his sister taking the plunge that put it into his mind!' Flora tried to speak lightly, although the news that Cissie was getting married was a surprise.

'That's nearer the mark than you realise.' Rab Lambie nodded. 'Cissie said it annoyed him when she decided to marry, and it was then he thought of you as a wife who would work and help his position in the business.'

'So it wasn't infatuation! Just looking after his own ends,' Aunt Isa declared. 'Always was a nasty specimen, even at school.'

'Ah, there's others who'd have jumped at the chance of marrying him,' Rab Lambie grunted gallantly. 'But Willie fancied having an attractive wife, too. And now, Isa — how about a cup of tea?'

Flora was puzzled as her aunt left the room, apparently flustered. Aunt Isa was usually the one in total control.

Rab Lambie told her about starting a cake and confectionery kiosk in the Byres Road branch, with either herself or her aunt to run it.

'But we'll decide which one of you when all this upset is just a memory.' He patted her hand reassuringly. There was a bluff kindliness about him which appealed to Flora. She wondered why her aunt disapproved of him.

★   ★   ★

By the middle of the afternoon Flora began to feel better, and was tempted to get up. But she knew it would annoy Aunt Isa if she didn't rest, so she stayed in bed, although she began to feel bored. In the late afternoon when the bell rang she was glad of the excuse to answer it. She gaped at the rounded, unkempt figure of Cissie Young on the threshold.

'Thought you were due an apology from the Young family,' she announced briskly, and came in, uninvited. 'Best get back to your bed.'

Flora led the way to her bedroom, feeling almost like giggling. It had been an amazing day for unexpected visitors.

Cissie settled herself beside the bed and gazed unabashed, at Flora's gashed face. 'My brother always had a temper, and he hates to be thwarted,' she declared. 'When he heard that Morgan Paton and myself were engaged to be married . . . ' She broke off. 'You remember Morgan Paton, the cobbler in Dumbarton Road?'

Flora nodded.

'He proposed on Hogmanay. William was furious and said he'd be getting married, too and mentioned you — thought he'd be getting himself a bargain.'

Cissie admitted she'd thought so, too, so it was a shock when Catriona McNeill revealed there was no engagement.

'I tackled him about it, and he went berserk denying it. That's when I knew it was all talk on his part. Pity, though! You might have made something of him,' Cissie remarked sadly. Then she perked up again, and chatted on at length, quietly jubilant that her brother had been summoned home by their seventy-year-old mother.

Flora remembered when the old lady ran the newsagent's — a wiry, formidable, black-clad figure, with grey hair scraped into a large bun at the back of her head and kept in place by ornate combs, which matched the dangling earrings she always wore.

'For years, my mother was on at William to get married — so she was really pleased when he said you were engaged, for she wants a grandchild. You'd have been just the right age,' Cissie observed regretfully, oblivious of the amazement on Flora's face.

'But it's me and Morgan who'll have to supply her with one — though I'm a bit long in the tooth, at thirty-eight.' Cissie sniffed noisily. 'Never mind, maybe you'll find a nice husband. After all, you're over ten years younger than me . . . '

Flora murmured her appreciation of the other woman's goodwill. 'And I take it that your brother will stop harassing me from now on?' she added.

'Take my word for it — I'm running the business now.' Cissie was decisive. She got up to go. 'Amazing who we end up with. Never thought Morgan Paton and I would make a pair. And my mother always says that eventually your Aunt Isa and Rab Lambie will be, too. After all, they were sweethearts in their schooldays.'

Flora gaped at this revelation. But that would explain why her aunt was so flustered and acted out of character when Rab was here. Why, then, did she always give the impression that she disapproved of him? And how about her fiancé, killed in the war, to whose memory she'd remained faithful, always wearing his ring?

Just before her aunt was due home, Flora got up, and met her fully dressed. She got her immediate attention by mentioning her last visitor.

Aunt Isa was relieved to hear Cissie Young had come to confirm her earlier news. Then, minutes later, Mona and Bartie arrived together to enquire how Flora was feeling.

Mona was delighted to see her on her feet, and looking better than when she left her that morning. Bartie could make no such comparison, seeing Flora's injuries for the first time.

'A terrible thing to have done to you!' He frowned, his good-natured face sterner than Flora would have thought possible. 'I've never lifted a hand in anger since I was a boy, nor has Hamish — but both of us this morning were prepared to give that Willie Young a hiding.'

'I'm glad it didn't come to that. His family have taken severe measures to curb him — and, anyway, I don't think he meant to injure me . . . ' Flora tried to be fair.

'Rubbish! It was a just a matter of time before this happened,' Aunt Isa snapped. 'You're a bit too forgiving for your own good, Flora.'

'And now you've all to come in to me for supper — I've got everything here.' Mona held up a bulging shopping bag. 'It's a double celebration — the King and Queen's Silver Jubilee, and I've heard from my father at last! So put on your war paint and come when you're ready.' She went next door, taking Bartie with her to help.

In her flat, he put a match to the fire which Catriona McNeill had left set and ready. Then, under Mona's guidance, he spread the kitchen table with a white, starched tablecloth and set it.

★ ★ ★

A little later Aunt Isa and Flora, carefully dressed, started across the landing to Mona's flat. They sat down at the table which was spread out invitingly, the late rays of the May evening sun slanting through the sparkling window glass on to it.

Mona set out to charm them all, for she wanted everyone in a good mood. After the meal, when the pleasant aroma of coffee filled the kitchen and everyone was happily relaxed and satisfied, Mona made her move.

'I'd love you all to come with me tomorrow afternoon to see Nadia. Last night Ralph Anderson suggested she would like some company. She isn't getting out now.'

'What you mean is you want me to

drive you there,' Bartie answered good humouredly.

'Yes, and I need Aunt Isa there, too. She has a rare gift for smoothing ruffled feelings — I want to make up with Loly again,' Mona confessed ruefully, and looked appealingly at Aunt Isa.

'I'm willing,' Aunt Isa agreed, smiling at how quickly she had become 'Aunt Isa' to the effervescent Mona. 'But four of us turning up uninvited might be imposing,' she added.

'Oh, no — I must go and let Nadia know I've had news from my father.' This was Mona's big dread — what if her stepmother had received no word? Nadia was especially vulnerable, too, since the baby was due next month.

On Sunday afternoon, before they set out, Mona spent half an hour creaming and powdering Flora's face until the discoloration was barely noticeable. Flora was delighted. If she could manage half as well herself, she could go to work tomorrow.

It was a pleasant May afternoon as they got into Bartie's car, the sun shone from a near-cloudless sky, and there was only the barest whisper of a breeze. The car cruised towards Pollokshields through tenement-lined streets, flags and bunting fluttering from the windows for the Silver Jubilee.

Down some side streets they saw the occupants had set out long tables for their street parties. Aproned housewives bustled to and fro, bringing plates of food from the houses, while the men carried down chairs and hordes of children ran around excitedly in the sunny weather.

Nadia was overjoyed when Mrs McLaurin showed them into the large plant-filled Victorian conservatory at the back of the house. She lay on a chaise-longue, wearing a loose black oriental kimono with a dragon embroidered on it, her dark hair Marcel-waved close to her head.

Ralph Anderson was sitting by her, and he rose to his feet.

'Oh, Mona, my dear, this is fortunate — I got a postcard from your father yesterday from some little village in France.' Nadia held it up excitedly. 'He says a letter will be following soon.'

Mona's face lit up with relief. 'So did I!' She gleefully pulled her postcard from her handbag and hurried over to embrace the reclining woman. Nadia looked well, although close up there was an air of sharp fragility about her face which the cosmetics could not hide.

Then Mona turned to the house-keeper, standing stiff and unsmiling by the door. 'And I've brought these for you, Loly — all your favourite cakes.'

Mona held out a daintily-tied box.

Mrs McLaurin stood unmoving for a long moment. 'I suppose this is a bribe to get on my good side,' she said, trying to sound severe.

'That's exactly what it is!' Mona cheerfully admitted, and threw her arms round the housekeeper and gave her a huge hug. 'You must come to see the flat.'

'Yes, it's been painted, papered and furnished,' Aunt Isa murmured. 'She's worked very hard. You should be proud of her.'

'Loly, I want you to see I'm no longer 'imperious, impetuous and impractical'.'

Mona planted a smacking kiss on the little housekeeper's face.

'Oh, you're just trading on my good nature. I'll come when I find time.' Mrs McLaurin extracted herself from the girl's embrace, but she was well pleased.

She was even polite to Bartie, Mona noticed. But then Bartie was looking distinguished today, in a well-tailored lounge suit, his sandy hair neatly brushed. Out of working hours, Bartie always dressed well. Only his hands betrayed that he was a working carrier.

Ralph Anderson looked almost insignificant beside him.

Mrs McLaurin brought in afternoon tea and took delight in presiding over it, gently pressuring Nadia to eat.

'Yes, I will try to eat something. Dr Anderson has just threatened that he might put me into hospital for the birth, and I don't want that. The child must be born here.'

'You have the option,' Ralph murmured. 'But I strongly recommend hospital. It would be a wise precaution taking into account all the modern advances we've made.'

Medical matters were not in Aunt Isa's opinion, suitable for polite conversation, so she was glad when Mona then started to regale them with her day in Lambies' kiosk, selling Jubilee cakes with red, white and blue favours. She could make the mundane sound amusing.

It was intriguing for Aunt Isa to watch Mrs McLaurin being solicitous towards Nadia. When she first met the little cook-housekeeper, she hadn't had a good word for her employer's wife.

She'd even blamed his disappearance on Nadia's extravagances.

Aunt Isa was quick to notice Flora standing with Ralph Anderson at the other end of the conservatory. Whatever he was saying, it was shocking Flora.

It was early evening when she, Flora, and Mona got back to her Shawlands flat and had a chance to talk over the afternoon's visit.

'Flora, what was young Dr Ralph so anxious to take you on one side and tell you about?' Mona asked suddenly.

Flora grimaced. 'The girl he wanted to marry got engaged to someone else on Friday night.' She explained how for years Ralph had worshipped Kirsty, and an understanding had grown between them. Now Ralph bitterly blamed himself. He'd chosen to go to the medical ball in Glasgow, instead of Kirsty's parents' silver wedding celebrations.

'Actually, he went as a career move. He wanted to buy a practice so that he could ask Kirsty to marry him,' Flora explained. 'But Kirsty was hurt, and thought he had put her second.'

Mona's soft heart was touched, but to their surprise Aunt Isa merely gave a snort of derision.

'He told you what his intentions were, but did he tell the girl? I doubt it!' she said curtly. 'I've no patience with men who leave the girl waiting, not quite sure where she stands. Rab Lambie did it to me, while he was getting the business started. We had a vague understanding, but he never proposed so he lost his chance.'

Flora listened, wide eyed, as Isa explained in a few nipped words how she had met her Robert, who declared his love, and they became engaged.

'Of course, Rab was hurt that I didn't wait till he was ready to ask. He's hardly given me a civil word since.' Aunt Isa closed her eyes and gave a ladylike shudder. 'Until yesterday on our way here. He said he thought I'd mourned Robert long enough, and it was time I married him!'

Flora and Mona stared open-mouthed at this. Neither could think of anything to say. They had thought prim Aunt Isa was the typical spinster.

'Is . . . is he like Willie Young, looking for a cheap shop assistant?' Mona asked eventually.

'Oh, no!' Aunt Isa shook her head. 'Wants me to take things easy, have a daily help and a maid — and for us to take a world cruise . . . ' She stopped, a little put out at having revealed so much.

'Sounds a nice prospect. He seemed the solid, steady type — like Bartie. Now if *he* was to offer me the same terms, I wouldn't hesitate,' Mona ended lightly.

It was not till next day at their tea-break that the two young women were able to discuss Aunt Isa's news.

'Who'd have thought Aunt Isa had a suitor in the wings!' Mona exclaimed. 'Wonder if she'll accept him?'

Flora shook her head, perplexed. Having lived quietly with her parents till so recently, she was at a loss. But the prospect was daunting. She'd just begun to enjoy her new life with Aunt Isa, after the upheaval of her father's death and the breaking up of her old home, and now . . .

'Did . . . did you mean it, when you said . . . about Bartie . . . ?' Flora asked hesitantly.

'Fat chance — Bartie is just building up his business. Doing his own carrying — everything from coal to furniture and grocery deliveries! All he could offer at the moment would be a rented single-end, or a room and kitchen! Imagine me!' Mona laughed merrily at the prospect.

That wasn't the reply Flora wanted. She genuinely wanted to know her friend's feelings towards Bartie, and Hamish, too — especially after the theatre invitation she'd received from him. After all, he had been Mona's boyfriend before her father's disappearance and the subsequent upheaval.

Flora wished she was more experienced in these matters, and envied her friend. Mona, five years her junior, had so much self-assurance where young men were involved.

'Hamish came to see me on Saturday morning,' Flora began, when Mona interrupted.

'Yes, isn't it wonderful about Donald John's interview with him today? I hope everything goes well and Donald John gets permanent employment. He's got a marvellous brain.'

Flora murmured her agreement, and went on doggedly. 'I mentioned I'd never been to the theatre, and Hamish said he'd get tickets for the Brandon-Thomas season.' She watched carefully for Mona's reaction.

'That's nice — but I doubt if his mother will allow it,' Mona remarked. 'She chases off any girl Hamish shows interest in. There were others before me, you know!'

Once Flora was back serving in the kiosk, she felt no further forward in finding out what regard Mona had for Bartie or Hamish, or more precisely, if there was one of them she preferred, and felt deeply about.

'I Won't Do It!'

Later, Flora looked up and found Mrs Buchanan, Hamish's mother, standing waiting to be served. It was Aunt Isa's lunch hour and Flora was on her own.

'My, what's happened to your face? Walk into a door?' Mrs Buchanan greeted Flora.

'Something like that.' Flora enquired how she could be of help.

'Don't worry, I know the whole story — met Cissie Young in Partick this morning,' Mrs Buchanan said triumphantly. 'No fool like an old fool trying to get himself a young wife.' She eyed Flora closely.

Flora's heart sank. She loathed being the subject of gossip, but knowing Cissie Young, the details would be all round Partick by now. But how could Mrs Buchanan, who lived in Cathcart, know Cissie?

Mrs Buchanan smiled indulgently at Flora, reading the question on her face. She leaned over the counter and whispered to her.

'Not many people know I do a few hours in a gown shop in Byres Road — helps eke out my army pension. Always get my husband's cigarettes and papers in Young's when I go to visit him. Cissie's served me for years.'

As she was speaking Flora could see Mona laughing in the glass-sided office above them, shaking a warning finger at her. It was a little confusing, since Mrs Buchanan was being friendly towards her.

Then she found out why.

'Hamish says he's taking you to the repertory season,' Mrs Buchanan said confidentially. 'I'd love to go, too! Always wanted to go to the Rep,' she declared. 'So my sister-in-law — you know, Bartie Darroch's mother — and myself are getting seats for the Brandon-Thomas season in the Royal.' She leaned forward confidentially.

'It'll have to be a Tuesday evening, since it's my half day, too. But we'll try to arrange our seats well away from you and Hamish. I wouldn't want to play gooseberry!' Mrs Buchanan whispered, beaming. 'That's what I came to explain . . . ' her voice rose to its usual blustering pitch. 'And since I'm here I'll take one of those fruit loaves and see if I can tempt my husband to eat a little.'

Flora wrapped up the purchase, avoiding looking at the glass-sided office where Mona was wagging a knowing finger. According to Mona, Mrs Buchanan chased away any girl in whom her only son showed interest.

Yet Flora didn't feel that she was being warned off. Mrs Buchanan seemed happy enough that Hamish had asked her to keep Tuesdays free to accompany him to the theatre. It was a kindly gesture made one Saturday when she was still reeling from the encounter with Willie Young.

Flora passed over the package. 'I hope your husband improves.'

'There's no betterment.' Mrs Buchanan sighed noisily. 'Amnesia — shell-shock, or whatever you like to call it — there's no medicine or surgery that can cure it. Some get better in time, but my Peter . . . ' She took her purchase and with a wave was gone.

At closing time Hamish was waiting outside the shop when Flora and Mona came out.

'How did Donald John come through the interview?' Mona asked.

'Old Mr McMorrin saw him, and he's on a week's trial. His writing should suit legal deeds very well,' Hamish said encouragingly.

Mona gave a whoop of delight. 'That's a relief! Must dash — got to see friends!' And with an airy wave she hurried away and left them together. It puzzled Flora. Mona had said she'd try out other make-up on her remaining bruises tonight.

Hamish turned to Flora. 'I've got seats for Emlyn Williams' play, 'Night Must Fall,' at the King's for tomorrow night, with Dame May Whitty, Angela Baddeley and Basil Radford. Did well in London, I believe.'

'Lovely!' Flora murmured. 'Your mother was in today and . . . '

'Yes.' Hamish grinned. 'They're going to the Royal. That's why I thought we'd go to the King's!'

Flora laughed outright, then stopped short. Just as her aunt was about to join her, Rab Lambie got out of a car at the kerb.

'Isa — could I see you for a minute?' He turned to Flora. 'Don't wait — I'll run Isa home later. And she'll have eaten.'

That evening Flora let herself into the Shawlands flat. She seldom came home on her own and it made her wonder about Mona's quick getaway.

Could she be unhappy, or even hurt, about Hamish's theatre invitation?

She never revealed her feelings now for her old boyfriend. It was a puzzle, for at times Mona seemed to want a special friendship with Bartie. Yet so far

217

they had never paired off or gone out together alone.

An uncertain chill fell on Flora. Suddenly she was strangely unsettled about the present situation. Perhaps it was just a mixture of fatigue, working so soon after the attack. And then there was the shock of hearing that Rab Lambie had proposed to Aunt Isa . . . on top of the nagging worry about the move to the Byres Road branch.

She dreaded that. It was so near her old home with its bittersweet memories — added to her nightmarish fear of meeting Willie Young again.

When Isa returned at almost eleven o'clock Flora was ready for bed.

'Och, that man!' Aunt Isa gasped as she came in the door. 'Never knew anyone so persistent. Look at the time — I should be in bed.' As she disappeared into her room, she saw the surprise on Flora's face. But how could she explain? She needed time to sort things out in her own mind.

Old feelings were stirring which she'd

thought long dead. It was a strange situation for a mature woman like herself to be in . . .

Flora stared at the closed door, longing to ask what Rab was persistent about. Was it wanting Aunt Isa to name the day? Or was he pressing her to make the move to his Byres Road branch? She went to bed, her head aching dully, her queries unanswered, and without having told her aunt about the theatre date with Hamish.

* * *

Flora met Hamish in town, and they went for high tea at Craig's tearoom in Gordon Street. Flora had never been there before and she enjoyed seeing the fine paintings on the wall in their large ornate frames.

Hamish was pleased that she approved. 'Mona never liked coming to this place — she said it looked too much like a gentleman's club!' he remarked and smiled. 'But Mona doesn't like plays very much, either. I took her to see Chekhov's 'Three Sisters.' She found it depressing and incomprehensible, and refused to go back to the Rep.' He laughed. 'She'd rather go to see Dave Willis doing his impersonation of Hitler at the Pavilion or the Mills Brothers at the Empire. She always says she'd rather be entertained than depressed!'

Somehow Hamish continuing to talk of Mona took the edge off Flora's enjoyment, and doubts were back gnawing at her self-esteem. Perhaps he was regretting his kind gesture, and would have preferred Mona here. But in the theatre she forgot her worries once the curtain was raised, and she was immersed in the plot as the chilling tale enfolded. The actors gave a reality to the story which a film could not have conveyed.

Her thoughts were still swimming when she left the theatre with Hamish. It was a jolt to be brought back to earth by Bartie's large figure, waiting for them in flour-covered overalls.

'Hamish — bad news. Your dad has had a seizure — your mother is at the hospital,' he said apologetically.

Flora saw the happiness drain from Hamish's face as he turned to her. 'I must go to the hospital.'

'I'll drop you off at the Victoria, and run Flora home,' Bartie offered. His cousin nodded wordlessly and the three of them got into Bartie's small car. There was little conversation during the journey and at the infirmary Hamish got out.

'Better not bank on next Tuesday,' he told Flora, sighing, and hurried off, his face grim.

'It's a disappointing end to your evening,' Bartie remarked. 'I'm sorry about this flour, by the way. It gets everywhere! But I worked on tonight to impress Rab Lambie. He's half promised me the contract to carry his dried goods — and that will be really worthwhile when the new branches open!'

'New branches?' Flora questioned.

Bartie glanced at her quickly. 'Didn't your aunt tell you?'

'No, but I guessed something was going on,' she reassured him. 'And don't worry, I won't mention it until it becomes official.'

'Thanks!' Bartie grinned. 'Would you like to have a quick look at the new premises I'm thinking of buying?'

'Love to!' Flora was pleased. She enjoyed hearing about Bartie's plans. He was so optimistic and enthusiastic.

Although she had lived in the South Side for some months now, she was still unfamiliar with all the side streets which branched off Victoria Road and Allison Street.

So it was interesting to watch Bartie as he turned into one then swung through a pend cut in the tenements to a group of buildings behind. They had obviously once belonged to a plumber's merchants, as rusting pipes and cracked sinks lay in the weed-covered yard.

Bartie had a key to the gate and

opened it and gave her a conducted tour.

'It needs a good clean before anything can be stored here,' Bartie admitted. 'But it is solid and watertight, and there's parking space for a few vans.'

Looking round, Flora remarked he would need to take on employees to make the extra space viable.

Bartie nodded agreement. 'At the moment I can afford to buy another van and take on an extra driver and labourer to help me,' he said. 'But I need bigger premises to expand — and it's a bit of a gamble, before I'm sure of the extra work.' He talked on about how well his plans had worked, and how pleased he was that his father had started to acknowledge his success.

She put out a hand and touched his sleeve. 'Bartie, you've worked wonders in eighteen months — but take care! Don't overdo it!'

He covered her hand with his and smiled. 'Thanks. No-one has ever noticed that I can get tired sometimes. I like it, coming from you.' He stood up. 'Come on, it's time we were both home.'

It was late when Flora put her key in the lock of Aunt Isa's flat that night, but the door opposite opened, and Mona came out.

'Enjoy it?' she asked.

'Marvellous!' Flora answered, then told her about Hamish's father.

'Oh dear, not another seizure!' Mona groaned. 'Hamish's father has had about half a dozen — most of them when he's been out with young ladies, including me.'

Mona saw Flora was shocked at her flippancy and rushed to explain. 'The poor man certainly has them, but I think dear Mrs Buchanan makes the most of them, to keep Hamish at heel.' Mona rushed on. 'Want to hear my news? Ralph Anderson was here tonight. He wants me to persuade Nadia to go into hospital for the baby.'

It took Flora a few moments to focus

her thoughts on this new information. 'Do you think you can manage to?' she murmured. 'Nadia seems so much against it.'

'She is!' Mona sighed. 'Feels her child will belong more to my father if it's born in the Pollokshields house. Strange sort of thinking, but she's determined.'

'But if Ralph feels she should go to hospital, it must be important,' Flora said seriously. 'He's a very caring doctor. His patients' well-being is paramount.'

'I'm not the one to persuade her, since I was born in the Pollokshields house — and I told him that. He thought perhaps you or Aunt Isa might try. She thinks a lot of you. You were the only one who took her seriously before she knew she was pregnant.'

'I couldn't possibly presume!' Flora was aghast at the thought.

'Exactly what I said to him,' Mona declared. 'And I told him it's time my father was informed. The lawyer should be told to contact him — at once! But Nadia doesn't want that, either.'

The weeks went by and Flora did not hear directly from Ralph, or Hamish, although news came to the shop that his father was holding his own. So much was going on in Lambies' that she didn't have time to dwell on either of them.

★ ★ ★

The truly unexpected happened when, late in the month, Aunt Isa announced that another assistant must be trained for the cakes and confectionery kiosk.

'It'll be difficult. I was lucky to get you,' Aunt Isa declared. 'We need a refined type of girl, who speaks well.'

Flora thought her aunt hadn't looked very hard. 'Would you consider Margaret Boulding?' she ventured, nodding to the grocery counter. Margaret had worked there since she left school at fourteen, and was the first female Mr

Hugh had allowed to be promoted to taking orders.

Isa Rennie was taken aback. Margaret hadn't come to her mind before. She considered her seriously, thinking of her family background. Respectable, hard-working folk. The father and the four girls paid the fees for the youngest boy to go to university, and become a teacher. Wonderful thing, a teacher in the family. And the girl was very like Flora; self-effacing, with a quiet dignity, and a very efficient assistant, too.

'Yes . . . ' Aunt Isa pondered. 'She might be exactly what we are looking for. And it'll serve Andy Rees right — he's put more and more on to Margaret lately, while he gossips in the back shop.

'And Flora, I want you to train her. In future I'll be dividing my time between here and the Byres Road branch, so you won't have to go there. Go now — Andy Rees isn't at the counter — find out if she's interested.'

Flora was stunned at the almost

off-hand way her aunt passed on this news. She wanted to ask more, but the finality in Aunt Isa's words deterred her.

There was a brief lull in customers and the counters were all free.

Dick, Harry and young Jamie Morton, behind the ham counter opposite, watched as she came out from the kiosk and went farther down the shop to grocery, which was on the curved horseshoe bend of the mahogany counter, immediately before the wines and spirits.

Margaret Boulding was measuring lentils into brown paper bags from the large sack at her feet, using a brass scoop. She was watching carefully for the swinging brass scale to level off, and didn't notice Flora for a moment.

'Margaret, how would you like promotion to the kiosk?' Flora asked, and explained about the new one being started in the Byres Road branch.

Surprise, mingled with apprehension, flitted over the other girl's face.

'Would . . . would I have to go to the West End?' Margaret asked tentatively. She'd lived in the South Side all her life, and for her, going over the Clyde to the other side of the city would be like travelling to a foreign country.

'Oh, no, you'll stay here,' Flora answered.

'Will I be allowed to wear a black dress and white collar, too?' Margaret's face was suffused with joy.

'Or a white blouse and skirt!' Flora replied.

'When do I start?'

'Immediately, if Mr Rees can spare you!'

'Oh, he'll make a fuss.' Margaret's shoulders sagged.

'I'll get Miss Rennie to speak to him,' Flora said. This would have to be done properly — one counter head approaching another. And Aunt Isa, the most senior assistant, held a special position in Lambies'.

But Flora did not have to approach her aunt, for just then, Rab Lambie came in. He spoke to Aunt Isa, then joined Flora at the grocery counter. Somehow, Andy Rees materialised immediately from the back shop, and was in position, smiling, when his employer arrived there.

Mr Lambie looked at the pink-faced girl behind the counter. 'You'll be Margaret Boulding?'

She nodded, her face getting pinker by the moment.

'Mr Rees, Margaret here is to be promoted to the fancy cake counter. Miss Flora Lochart will train her. See Mr Hugh about getting a replacement.'

Flora marvelled at the decisive way Mr Lambie made his wishes known, so that with no argument or debate Margaret became an assistant on Aunt Isa's special counter.

In the back shop Margaret did a little dance of joy. 'What luck that Mr Lambie came in! Otherwise old Rees would have hummed and hawed, and mightn't have allowed me to make the change.'

Flora knew it was true. All the counter heads were very touchy about their position, and guarded their privileges accordingly.

From the office, Mona saw the girls smiling happily as Margaret took off her white overall, apron and mob cap. She came down the stairs, eager to find out what was happening, and was thunderstruck when Flora told her.

'Flora, you're being allowed to train someone for the great kiosk just like that? When you started just a few months ago you weren't allowed to serve an account customer for weeks!'

'I can hardly believe it myself!' Flora nodded.

But Margaret's eyes were shining with happiness about her promotion.

'Just think! I won't have to brush out this back shop and put down fresh sawdust every morning. It was always done by the message boys till old Rees volunteered me a couple of years ago. Just did it to keep me in my place when I was promoted to orders.'

There were few female assistants in Lambies'. It was the policy to have men in all the counter positions, except for the cake kiosk.

When Margaret was allowed to take phone orders and make them up, it caused some resentment, although she was more efficient than anyone else in the shop.

Bartie came into the back shop carrying a large box of tinned goods. He saw Margaret with Flora and Mona.

'The usual place for these?' he said to her.

Margaret nodded, and rushed to tell him her news.

'You deserve it!' he said, giving her back a little pat.

★　★　★

Bartie unbuttoned his brown coat overall, revealing a well-cut lounge suit underneath. 'I'm seeing the Lambie brothers about extra carrying work,' he explained to Flora.

'How is Hamish's father?' she inquired.

'He's rallied again, but . . . ' he shrugged his shoulders. 'I think it's Aunt Maisie's will that keeps him alive.' He looked at Flora. 'You're better. Fully recovered?' he asked gently.

'Yes, just a tiny cut on the bridge of my nose left.' Flora smiled. So much had happened in Lambies' that concern about her injuries had receded into the background.

'Now the Rep season has finished, I see 'The Half Past Eight Show' has started again for the summer. That's at the King's. 8.30 is a good time for me — maybe — maybe on Tuesday we could go?' Bartie ventured.

'Oh, yes — let's! Mona loves that kind of show,' Flora cried delightedly, and then stopped, as she noticed Bartie looking at her strangely.

Suddenly it dawned on her that he had only been inviting her!

But at that moment Rab Lambie came through to the back shop.

'Perhaps since his father is a little better, Hamish will come and make the foursome,' Bartie said hastily. 'I'll contact you.' And he went forward and shook Rab's hand.

Feeling a little foolish at her thoughtless mistake, Flora hurried back to the kiosk and found Aunt Isa serving Mrs McLaurin.

The little housekeeper was shaking her head dolefully.

'Nadia isn't as well as she makes out. And young Dr Anderson is trying to get her to book into one of the big nursing homes or, better still, Redlands Hospital for Women, but she won't listen to him. I've tried to make her see sense. After all, she's old for having her first baby — but she tells me I don't know what I'm talking about, since I've never had any children.'

Aunt Isa made soothing noises, and sent the little woman out feeling that she was doing her best.

Flora had never seen Mrs McLaurin look so morose and dispirited and this, added to Ralph's concern about Nadia, made her very uneasy. She knew he was always coolly objective in his medical judgment.

* * *

That evening when they got home, they found Ralph Anderson waiting for them on the landing.

'How's Nadia?' Mona asked at once.

'Still a lady in waiting,' Ralph said with a small smile. 'But that could change in hours, or days . . . '

'Weeks?' Mona queried.

He shrugged. 'Yes, but it's an outside chance — babies are very unpredictable. Personally, I would say a day or two, at the most.' He paused, his eyes on Mona. 'Could I have a private word with you? And then I'd like to see you, Flora.'

Inside Mona's flat, the fire was set, but the evening was warm. She didn't light it. Ralph sat down and came to the point at once.

'Your stepmother won't allow your father to be sent for, but she has agreed that the moment the baby is born the lawyer can contact him with the news.' He sighed. 'It's the best I can do. I don't want to pressure her, because that might upset her. And that's the worst thing for her at the moment.'

Mona nodded. In retrospect, she was sure that her stepmother's first months of pregnancy had somehow contributed to her father's disappearance. She recalled thinking then that Nadia had undergone a change. Suddenly, she'd become irritable, moody and noisily temperamental. Round about then was the first time she had ever heard her mild-mannered father raise his voice.

'Is there anything I can do?' she asked.

'Yes — go back and live with her till after the baby's born.'

Mona jumped to her feet. 'Did Nadia put you up to this?'

'No.' He answered, 'Although she wants it. Personally I would like both you and Mrs McLaurin there, especially at night. I have my other patients, and can't be with her twenty-four hours a day.'

Mona sank down into her chair again and looked around the cosy little flat she'd made her own. She didn't want to leave — she loved it. Here, she felt in control of her life for the first time.

'The truth is that I'm not sure how Mrs McLaurin will act in a crisis. She does a lot of talking, but I've the feeling that on her own, she might panic and be useless. And there don't seem to be any other relatives, except yourself,' Ralph said seriously.

Mona recognised his point. Loly was full of bluster and good intentions, but she was inclined to run away from emergencies. Like the time one of their maids fell downstairs and injured her head. Mona was only sixteen at the time but she'd had to phone the doctor and get an ambulance.

'All right!' Mona sighed. 'When do you want me to go?'

'At once,' he answered. 'I'll take you there after I've spoken to Flora. Give you time to pack.'

After he rang, Flora opened the door. Ralph explained about waiting for Mona and spoke to her on the landing. 'I've been invited to a senior doctor's home next Tuesday evening. He's offering me part of his practice, and I need a partner. Will you help me out?'

Something prompted Flora to be cautious, but she answered truthfully.

'I'm sorry, I've made arrangements for next Tuesday.' She knew she could see Bartie tomorrow, and he wouldn't have had time to book their theatre seats, but somehow she didn't want to. It surprised her. Time was when she'd have jumped at the opportunity.

He looked crestfallen. 'Please, can't you cancel?' he said urgently. 'This is a fantastic chance, and it came right out of the blue. You remember Dr Elliot Weir and his wife? I introduced you to them the night of the medical ball. They were very taken with you.'

Flora remembered the hearty grey-haired doctor and his wife, and the roguish compliments to 'Ralph's young lady.' It had been embarrassing.

'But I think they — I mean — he thought that . . . we . . . I was . . . ' Flora tried to put it delicately, but Ralph did not help her, and she finished bluntly. 'I think he mistook me for Kirsty.'

'Is that such a bad thing? After all, we've known one another for a long time. And these past few months you've blossomed into a most attractive young woman,' Ralph murmured, a little smile on his lips.

Flora looked at him in amazement, gradually realising what he was saying. As a student, Ralph had been like a brother, confiding in her his love for Kirsty. But now Kirsty was to marry someone else . . .

'Yes, we could make a very nice couple,' Ralph said complacently.

She stiffened. He seemed so sure of her, but she was no longer the gauche girl who was flattered to share his company any time he felt like dropping in.

'No, Ralph! I won't do it! And you have absolutely no right to assume that I would!'

Ralph's News

Next morning Mona bounced into the shop, her blonde curls dancing round her face. She was feeling virtuous and at peace with the world, having returned to stay at her old home until her stepmother's confinement.

At the cake kiosk she stopped, and looked quizzically at Flora.

'Lunch is on me today — you have to spill the beans about Ralph. What did you do to make him so dejected last night?' Then she was off to the office, her high-heeled shoes clicking over the marble of the shop floor.

Flora hid her consternation. The last thing she wanted was to discuss her meeting with Ralph, especially as he was Nadia's doctor. The longer she reflected on his strange proposal, the more upset she got. It was plain he saw her merely as an aid to further his career, and she resented it. If he'd even mentioned having some regard for her, she wouldn't feel so bad. But then, how could he, after the hours he'd spent telling her about Kirsty?

Margaret Boulding was beside Flora, wearing a simple black dress, with a string of pearls at the neck.

She was quick to learn the ways of the kiosk. To Flora, when she started six months ago, it was all new and frightening. She was relieved that Aunt Isa was not here overseeing her first morning of being fully in charge. It was humbling enough to see how competently Margaret served customers, even on this busy Saturday morning. But she felt a little better when Margaret confided in her later.

'I'm glad you're training me. With Miss Rennie I'd have been all fingers and thumbs — probably stuttering to the customers as well!'

At lunch-time Mona and Flora met in the local Home Bakeries. At once

Mona inquired about the kiosk's new assistant.

'It's a bit chastening to be able to leave her on her first day — and a Saturday, at that! It was weeks before Aunt Isa left me,' Flora answered with a rueful laugh.

'She's a trained assistant — it's just another counter for her.' Mona shrugged, then asked eagerly about Flora's encounter with Ralph the evening before.

Flora tried to be off-hand. 'He needed a partner for Tuesday evening,' she murmured, and explained about having already agreed to go to the theatre with Bartie that night. But she couldn't put into words the marriage proposal inherent in Ralph's invitation. Somehow, that had outraged her. It seemed insulting, coming so soon after Kirsty had jilted him.

'Oh, is that all!' Mona said. 'He seemed quite put out.'

To avoid talking about Ralph, Flora

asked how Mona enjoyed being back in her old home.

'I'd scarcely arrived before I began to wonder if Ralph really wanted me there as a referee between Loly and the nurse!' Mona laughed.

'Nurse?' Flora questioned.

'Oh, yes. Nadia has a full-time nurse living in.'

Flora was silent, surprised. Why, then, was Mona needed there, too?

'Can Nadia afford a nurse?' Flora queried after a little.

'Just what I asked.' Mona nodded. 'I mean, Ralph has his own midwife. But guess what I discovered? Nadia is comfortably off in her own right. Her people were pawn-brokers in a big way, and she has a thousand guineas a year, for a start.'

Secretly Mona wondered if this was perhaps another reason contributing to her father's departure. Did Nadia lay down conditions? Maybe he wouldn't live on her money! Bit by bit Mona felt she was finding out about her father's planned disappearance . . .

Meanwhile Flora was bewildered that anyone could have an income of twenty pounds a week. It was three times what a doctor earned, five times a top tradesman's wage and ten times what she earned in Lambies', even after her huge ten-shilling rise.

Mona saw Flora's perplexed look and launched into a funny description of the feud between the nurse and the little housekeeper.

' . . . then last night, Nurse Laidlaw caught Loly giving Nadia her evening toddy to help her sleep. Absolutely threw a fit!' Mona laughed. 'I got the feeling Nadia quite enjoys them fighting over her . . . Somehow, although she's old enough to be my mother, she seems curiously immature . . . '

'I was told the pair of you were here!' Bartie's voice interrupted.

'Come and join us!' Mona invited brightly, indicating the third chair at their table. 'Sorry I can't come on Tuesday evening. Promised to stay in nights and keep Nadia company.' She stood up, lifting her handbag and gloves. 'And I'm afraid I've got to leave now — have to get a few things for Nadia.' With an airy wave, she strolled out, every eye in the tea-room following her.

'Hamish isn't free on Tuesday, either. You can still go, I hope?' Bartie said quickly.

'Oh, yes, I wouldn't miss it!' Flora smiled. 'What show is it?'

'It's something new. 'The Half Past Eight Show' has just one house, and I hear the sets are sophisticated and lavish, like the films.'

'Sounds exciting! I'm glad you asked me,' Flora exclaimed.

'I've wanted to ask you out since we first met, the day of your interview,' he admitted. 'But then, I thought you and Hamish . . . at least, I thought he was keen . . . '

'Hamish and I discuss books and plays — but he's Mona's friend,' Flora admitted.

Bartie smiled back, his hand reaching out to cover hers. 'Good!'

Flora went back to the shop in a daze. It was pleasant to be sought after.

She didn't see Aunt Isa that day in Lambies', and was asleep before she came home in the evening. It was becoming a familiar routine these days, Flora thought. Now they seemed to communicate by scribbled notes and seldom had the opportunity to talk.

★　★　★

Next day, Sunday, was the monthly family lunch day, at Robert and Milly's new bungalow in Clarkston.

When Flora got there the garden still looked like a building site, but inside the house was perfection itself.

Milly and Robert appeared suddenly younger, the tenseness which was always around them now eased. Milly was quite girlish in her enthusiasm, conducting Flora and Sally round the four-roomed bungalow.

'Look at the kitchen — two good delph sinks, and a gas boiler right next to them. Makes washday so easy!' Milly enthused.

'You've been very sensible with the book money,' Sally remarked glumly. 'George bought a few dental instruments and we got bikes for the boys, but it mostly just seemed to melt away.'

Flora tried to hide the pang this gave her. Her father's books had been so precious to him. That money from their disposal should have been frittered away really hurt. But then, Sally always was extravagant. 'I'm glad you've got your dream house,' she told Milly.

'It's made such a difference now Robert has to travel home instead of just running upstairs to the flat. Most of the time he used to work on in the bank, but now he can't wait to get home to clear the garden!'

The meal was excellent. Milly was so happy with the bungalow that Flora found herself almost liking her. Even her waspish tongue seemed to have changed, at least for today.

Later, as she was leaving, it surprised her when Robert drew her aside.

'I was speaking to Ralph Anderson during the week. Did I get the right impression that you and he are . . . ?' Robert sought for the right word.

'No, we aren't walking out together,' Flora answered sharply.

Robert was surprised by her blunt retort. Flora was usually so calm and even tempered.

'We . . . at least, Milly and I are very grateful to him,' Robert said cautiously. 'If he hadn't told me Dad's books were valuable we wouldn't have this place. And Ralph did speak so highly of you.'

On top of the tram going home to Shawlands, Flora seethed quietly.

Why should Ralph imply there was a romantic attachment between them? To him, she was merely the one he turned to when he was in a jam.

She sighed. Was there another girl in Glasgow who'd got two proposals because she would be a help?

On Tuesday morning Mona did not appear for work and there was speculation that Nadia's baby was on its way. The day wore on with no news, and Flora felt anxious.

But the lavish show that evening in Bartie's comforting company banished her uneasiness. At the end, as she waited in the crowded foyer for him to collect his coat, a little wiry old woman with dangling earrings suddenly appeared directly in front of her.

Flora's mind was awash with the colourful scenes from the show, and she didn't recognise Willie Young's mother for a moment.

'Well, you've done well for yourself. Quite the mannequin! Great what the bit of money from your father has done for you,' Mrs Young declared sourly, eyeing the smart outfit Flora wore. 'Soon made you break your word to my Willie. Maybe he shouldn't have touched you, but he was provoked.'

Flora stood, rooted to the spot, as the little woman justified her son's actions.

It seemed she had now convinced herself that Flora had accepted his proposal. Then, as if drawing courage from his mother, Willie Young came forward, grinning at Flora's discomfort.

But he soon shrank back as Bartie's large figure appeared beside her, and gasped as he found his arm in Barties' blood-stopping grip.

'Stay away from this young lady!' Bartie hissed.

'Excuse me, sir, are these people bothering you?' The uniformed commissionaire interrupted Bartie.

He glared suspiciously at the Youngs, the old bare-headed woman who looked like a ragwife, and the unkempt, podgy man beside her. They were not the type who normally frequented the main foyer of the theatre.

'We paid our money!' Mrs Young muttered, then turned to her son. 'You're well rid of her!' And she pushed her way through the waiting crowd, some of whom had been watching with interest. Her son slunk off behind her.

Flora was shaken — she hated being the centre of a scene.

Bartie took her arm and guided her to his car. He didn't drive off immediately, but exploded with anger. 'That fellow has to be stopped from pestering you!'

'It wasn't him this time — it was his mother.' Flora sighed.

They drove to Shawlands in silence. It was difficult to explain to Bartie that because she now dressed fashionably, and had had her hair styled, Mrs Young could believe Willie's lies.

Bartie hadn't known her before she came to live with Aunt Isa.

★ ★ ★

When they got home, Flora was pleased to find her aunt there. Aunt Isa insisted it was an occasion for a celebratory glass of sherry. It jolted Flora out of her anxiety, especially when the display cabinet was unlocked and her grandmother's best crystal glasses were brought out.

'Here's to many pleasant evenings!' Bartie toasted them and looked at Flora with a cheerful grin, before he took his first sip.

Aunt Isa laid her glass down carefully and cleared her throat. 'I think it's time you knew, Flora, that I've been involved in the negotiations with Rab over his purchasing the Westergait Licensed Grocers.'

'The Westergait shops!' Flora exclaimed. She didn't think these small grocers would interest Lambies'. There were at least half a dozen branches around Glasgow — small, single shops with the grocery side of the business down one wall, large cheeses and bulk butter cheek by jowl with hams and cooked meats and tinned goods. Along the opposite wall was the licensed trade counter, barrels of whisky, sherry and port, the taps dripping on to the sawdust-covered floors.

'They're not in Lambies' class, and they've been allowed to deteriorate. An old story — the owner became his own best customer at the whisky barrel.' Aunt Isa sighed.

'Is the sale definite?' Flora asked.

'Yes, indeed! All signed and sealed today.' Aunt Isa turned to Bartie. 'Quite a coincidence — your cousin, Hamish, is the lawyer acting for Westergait. He's been working on the sale, hunting up title deeds and whatnot for the last few weeks.' She turned triumphantly to Flora. 'And Bartie's got the job of doing all the carrying between the branches.'

Flora murmured a suitably surprised comment, avoiding Bartie's twinkling eyes. Aunt Isa explained that the counter heads in Lambies' were to be offered promotion to become managers in the new branches. And the younger men in Lambies' were to take over their positions.

There was a sudden jangle of the bell in the lobby, and Aunt Isa hurried to answer the door. Flora and Bartie exchanged mystified looks when they heard Hamish's voice. It was not the time of night for a social call.

Aunt Isa led him into the room. 'Hamish is here — Mona phoned him. Flora, she wants you to go to the Pollokshields house.'

'Mona is upset,' Hamish explained. 'I don't think things are going smoothly, and she needs your support, Flora.'

★ ★ ★

In the Pollokshields mansion, the day had begun happily. Nadia's labour started, to her great delight, and she begged Mona to stay. But as the hours went by, gradually she became more and more agitated. She clung piteously to Mona's presence, not wanting her to leave, even with the doctor, nurse and midwife there. It was a situation that Mona had never experienced, and she felt unsure of how to help.

Then, in late afternoon, Ralph informed her that he was bringing in a consultant. Within minutes of Mr McKay arriving, the decision was taken to operate.

The kitchen table was manhandled upstairs to the bedroom, while Mona and Mrs McLaurin stayed, shocked, in the kitchen. They knew it must be serious. It was then that Mrs McLaurin started to keen, rocking herself back and forward in her chair, and throwing her apron over her head.

Old memories suddenly flooded back to Mona of the night her mother died. Loly had acted just like this. As a fifteen-year-old she had stood, watching in horror, until her father came in and gently ushered her out.

Now Mona longed to have Flora here. Living all her life in a close-knit tenement community, Flora had experience of this kind of situation. She would know what to do now.

So Mona phoned Hamish, and asked him to get Flora for her.

'Is there anything I can do?' Hamish asked gently.

Mona closed her eyes tightly for a moment to stop the tears which jumped to her eyes at the tender note in his voice.

Normally she would have given a cutting reply but she was exhausted emotionally and physically.

'I don't know! I just don't know!'

'Don't worry, then — I'll get Flora for you,' Hamish assured her.

Just as she put the phone down, Ralph came downstairs. He looked pale and strained. 'It's a boy — pretty weak, I'm afraid. And your step-mother ... we can hardly get a pulse.'

'You've done all you could — and more,' Mona said gently. Till that moment Ralph had seemed a cold, clinical person she didn't like very much. Today that had changed, and she saw him as someone to admire and respect.

'Could you be there if she comes round?' he asked.

Mona stared at him, panic rising within her at the wording of his request. '*If* she comes round.' It took a superhuman effort of will to follow him back upstairs.

Nadia was lying in bed, white faced, with her eyes closed. The midwife sat on a small stool nearby, cradling the baby.

'Here's the bairn,' she said to Mona in a matter-of-fact voice. 'Got hair the colour of yours.'

Nadia's eyes flickered open. It took her a moment to focus on Mona.

'Is it a boy?' she asked in a whisper.

Mona nodded, and stood back to allow the midwife to show Nadia her son. She gave a weak little laugh. 'I'm glad he's got your hair. He's your little brother. A real Alexander . . . ' Then her eyes closed and she seemed to drift off again.

Mona looked towards Ralph and the specialist, who were standing at the foot of the bed, and they motioned her to stay.

Then Nadia's eyes opened again and she spoke in a barely-audible voice. 'Mona . . . Mona . . . look after him

. . . love him . . . '

'No!' Mona almost shouted. '*You* must look after him. He needs you . . . you've got to fight!'

'I'll try,' Nadia whispered.

★　★　★

A little later Bartie's car drew to a stop outside the gates, and Flora and Hamish got out. Mona opened the door to them, and fell into Flora's arms. She sobbed for a few moments, hugging her tightly, then pushed herself away. 'I'm so grateful to you both.' She nodded to each of them. 'Nadia's very poorly. The baby had to be delivered by an emergency Caesarean operation. Ralph says he's weak, too.'

Flora and Hamish followed her through into the cluttered kitchen at the back of the house. Mrs McLaurin was sitting hunched in the front of the big four-oven range, running her hand back and forth along the hem of her apron. She stared into the dying fire and didn't look up.

Flora guessed at once that she was probably Mona's main problem at the moment.

'Loly, we could do with some tea and toast,' Mona said, going over to her and shaking her shoulder.

'How can you think of food and drink when there's death in this house tonight?' Mrs McLaurin said mournfully.

'It hasn't come to that yet!' Ralph's voice interrupted sharply from the door. 'And tea and toast would be most welcome. My midwife and Nurse Laidlaw could certainly do with some.' He spoke with authority, and Mrs McLaurin looked up, startled out of her lethargy. 'Immediately!' he ordered.

She got up reluctantly and began laying out cups. Flora slipped off her coat and started to help.

'Miss Alexander — Mona — your father ought to be contacted immediately. The child has a chance, but your stepmother's life is on a very slender thread,' Ralph said quietly.

'I'll contact your lawyer, Mr Grant, at home,' Hamish offered at once and Mona nodded in dumb agreement.

Hamish put an arm about her shoulder and drew her out to the telephone in the hall. When the tray was ready, Flora carried it upstairs for the two nurses, and sat with Nadia while they had their tea and toast.

When she got back to the kitchen Ralph was sitting at the kitchen table, his head buried wearily in his hands.

'Mr Grant has been. They're trying to telegraph Paris,' he said quietly, without looking directly at her.

'I'm sorry Nadia didn't listen to you and go to hospital for the baby,' Flora murmured.

Ralph shrugged. 'Don't know if it would have made a great deal of difference, as things worked out.' He got to his feet. 'Must get back to my patient.' He went quickly out of the room, without once looking at her. He had treated her like a stranger.

Flora felt unreasonably hurt. But then, what could she expect? He had proposed, albeit in a strange way, and her refusal was very blunt. Perhaps it was best this way. Yet it rankled — they had known one another for a long time, and his friendship was important to her.

Mona came back, Hamish solicitously by her side. She sat down at the table with a helpless little laugh. 'I should have realised — my father has been staying with old friends in Paris all this time, the first place I should have thought of! We always stayed there.' Mona shook her head at her own stupidity. 'He hadn't really disappeared.'

Flora poured tea and made them sit down and take it and the toast.

The phone soon rang and Mona sprang up and rushed out into the hall. She was back in a moment and held up a piece of paper she had written on. 'That was a telegram. Dad's coming home!'

The news that her employer was on his way home seemed to galvanise Mrs McLaurin into action, although each movement was punctuated with deep sighs.

It was late next day when Flora got to Lambies'. She had taken a turn sitting with Nadia, and it was six in the morning before she got to bed.

Ralph stayed most of the night, too, but Flora felt curiously shut out as he treated her distantly, like a stranger. She found she desperately wanted back to their old footing when they chatted freely.

'Did you enjoy your date with Bartie?' Margaret Boulding asked during a lull in serving.

'Oh, yes!' Flora smiled. 'So much happened afterwards, though, it rather put it out of my mind.'

'A night out with Bartie would be the highlight of my life,' Margaret said lightly. And Flora knew she meant it, too.

Mona's absence seemed to dampen

everyone's spirits. Usually, during the day, she was up and down the wooden steps, with cheerful quips for everyone.

Bartie came in on his usual daily deliveries. He was anxious to fix another evening out with Flora, and seemed a little put out when she declined. She wanted to be with Mona during the next few days, remembering too well the trauma of her own parents' illnesses.

Flora stayed overnight again with Mona in Pollokshields.

She noticed at once, despite Nadia's unchanged condition, the house seemed more ordered.

'Catriona McNeill has come and tidied the place up,' Mona explained with a small smile. 'She was once maid to a titled lady, so Loly has accepted her. They've been swapping stories in the kitchen.'

Mona's problems filled Flora's thoughts so it startled her when she arrived at Lambies' in the morning to find the staff in a state of excitement.

Margaret thrust a newspaper into her hands, excitement in her voice.

'Says Rab Lambie has bought the Westergait shops — and he will be marrying his longest serving employee, Miss Isa Rennie!'

Hugh Lambie would not comment, so all the staff waited for Flora to confirm the news, and give them more details. But she just had to shrug her shoulders and explain she knew no more than was in the papers.

★　★　★

In the evening it was a titbit of news which took Mona's mind off her worries. It amazed, yet appealed to her that confirmed spinster Aunt Isa should have a romantic interlude in her life.

Mona's problems soon loomed once more when Ralph came into the kitchen to tell them Nadia's condition had deteriorated. Flora stayed with Mona in the sickroom, until the door opened and a tall, slightly stooped man entered.

She knew at once this was Mona's father, Stuart Alexander.

As father and daughter greeted one another, and he was shown the tiny scrap of life which was his son, Flora got up quietly and left.

Mrs McNeill was staying to help Mrs McLaurin, so Flora decided to go home. Ralph came downstairs as she was making for the front door.

'Leaving?' he asked.

'Yes. Mona and her father have a lot of catching up to do, and there are two women in the kitchen for the practical work. I'll go home and see if Aunt Isa really has named the day!' she finished lightly, pleased that he was standing talking, and not turning away.

'I'll run you home. It's raining. It won't take five minutes,' he said, as she made to refuse.

As his car drew up at the close he spoke. 'Last time I did this Willie Young was waiting upstairs.'

Flora shuddered. 'I saw him on Tuesday night, with his mother. She's obviously convinced I turned him down when better things came on the horizon.'

'That couldn't be true. You are completely honest, and not the slightest bit devious,' he said quietly. 'By the way,' he added. 'I'm moving out of general practice, and specialising. I've decided to take the hospital post under Mr McKay.'

'I didn't know you'd got another offer!' Flora exclaimed.

'I had it before Dr Weir's, but his offer had a nice little house with it, and I thought suddenly of being married to you. It all seemed very attractive.' He sighed. 'Strange, how you never see something or someone . . . take things for granted . . . ' He rubbed his hand over his eyes. 'Fatigue lets the defences down. Sorry!' He leaned over and opened her door.

Flora scrambled out and watched as he drove off quickly.

'Talking Of Weddings . . .'

The electric ceiling fans whirred constantly and kept the interior of Lambies' shop slightly cooler than the streets outside. In front of the windows, the canvas sunshades were fully extended as the staff battled to keep their produce fresh and cool.

Heatwaves in July were a nightmare. Cheeses began to sweat, butter to melt, and the icing and chocolates in the kiosk became soft and lost their gloss.

Most of the perishable stock was put in the cool room, a large, tiled, windowless larder in the back shop. The staff made extra journeys to it and brought out small quantities at a time.

Flora and Margaret in the kiosk were flushed from running back and forth to replenish their stock.

★ ★ ★

Mid-morning, Flora stifled a groan as the large, determined figure of Mrs Buchanan, Hamish's mother, made for the kiosk. She was the last customer Flora wanted in this sultry weather. She forced a smile and politely inquired after Mrs Buchanan's war-wounded husband.

'He's rallied again, out of bed, and even lucid at times. Strange thing, the mind,' she answered heartily. 'Is Mona Alexander in?'

So Mona was the reason for Mrs Buchanan's visit.

'She's still at home, but she's hoping to be back in a day or two,' Flora murmured.

'I suppose you know she's got my Hamish running after her again like a little lapdog!' Mrs Buchanan snapped.

'He was a great help to Mona in contacting her father.' Flora strove to keep her voice mild.

'Yes, I hear Nadia Alexander was at death's door after the birth. But that young doctor friend of yours brought her back to life, so they say!' Mrs Buchanan sniffed. 'High and mighty, that one. Used to be sweet on a girl from Ayrshire. She broke off her engagement last week over him — and now he doesn't want to know! Going to become a great surgeon, or some such nonsense.' Mrs Buchanan waved a hand dismissively.

This news startled Flora. Ralph had yearned after Kirsty from his student days. Her recent hasty engagement had hurt him deeply.

Yet how could Mrs Buchanan know about Kirsty, who lived in Ayrshire? But then — minding other people's business was Mrs Buchanan's hobby.

Flora waited tensely to hear more, but Mrs Buchanan changed the subject.

'I really thought you and Hamish were becoming good friends.' She watched Flora closely. 'Or is my nephew Bartie the attraction for you?'

'I'm equally friendly with them both,' Flora murmured, trying to smile. 'And now what can I do for you?' She deliberately changed the conversation this time. Mrs Buchanan only came into Lambies' when she wanted information.

'Oh, one of those fruit loaves I got last time,' she said dismissively. 'I heard Stuart Alexander, Mona's father, came home right away?'

'Yes, his presence as much as anything helped Nadia, although she's not out of the wood yet. It's only just over two weeks since the baby was born.'

'And my Hamish has been at that house every moment he can spare!' Mrs Buchanan dabbed at little beads of perspiration on the bridge of her nose then took the plunge. 'Do you know if there's anything between Hamish and Mona Alexander? Are they talking of anything . . . ?'

'I don't know. I haven't been up to the house very often since the baby was born,' Flora answered truthfully.

Mainly, she stayed away because she dreaded meeting Ralph there, and she despised herself for being such a coward. Since he'd dropped her at her close the day after the baby's birth, her mind had been in a turmoil. For him to admit she had become very dear to him upset her.

'Of course, you wouldn't tell — after all, you're her friend.' Mrs Buchanan banged a silver threepenny piece on the counter, swiped the ha'penny change out of Flora's hand and stamped out of the shop.

'Never seen you annoyed before!' Margaret breathed admiringly.

'It's so trying — the heat — and a prickly customer, on top of everything else this morning,' Flora said, sighing.

Margaret nodded. Since the news that interviews for promotion to the new branches were to be that afternoon, there were tensions, and even intrigues, within Lambies'.

Then there was Bartie arriving first thing this morning with a delivery, when she and Flora were still in the back shop.

'We've hardly seen you!' Margaret chided him.

'Yes. I've been working day and night, settling into the new premises, and taking on three employees,' he answered with satisfaction. 'Hope you've missed me, Flora?'

Flora looked up from checking stock. It was the first morning in almost two weeks that Bartie had taken time to give them more than a cheerful wave in passing.

'It's certainly an important time for you,' she answered non-committally.

'Yes, my father will have to admit now that I'm successful,' Bartie rubbed his hands in satisfaction. 'And one more thing would complete my happiness. Flora — will you walk out with me? We could make it official.'

Flora's mind was still half occupied with the stock, and it was a moment before she realised what Bartie was asking in such a matter-of-fact fashion.

She felt cornered, and embarrassed. Margaret was looking on, open mouthed in surprise at Bartie's words.

The truth was Flora had not missed Bartie. Her thoughts had been elsewhere. 'Thank you for asking,' she said with a faint smile, 'but I'm too set in my ways — not the right person for you at all.'

Bartie's face fell with disappointment and Flora almost relented, hating to hurt this big, good-natured man.

'Oh, well, if that's the way of it . . . ' Bartie shrugged sadly, and went off slowly to finish his delivery.

★   ★   ★

Margaret avoided Flora's eyes. She wished Bartie had asked her. He was one of the reasons she had jumped at the chance to work in the kiosk. She'd longed to get out of the overalls and mob-cap, and wear a dress so that Bartie might notice her.

Margaret admitted to herself that she was bored. It had only taken her a day to master the kiosk skills, and now she missed the variety of her old job on groceries. Without false modesty, she knew that she was the person to take over the grocery counter if Andy Rees got moved to one of the Westergait shops.

'Do you ever get fed up doing this job?' she asked a little later.

The question surprised Flora. 'No! I was so grateful to get the kiosk, at my age and untrained,' she answered, still remembering the early morning shift in Young's newsagent's, especially in winter. But it made her wonder if there was enough challenge for an experienced assistant like Margaret.

Such thoughts were swept from her mind as she found herself looking at Cissie Young. Her hair was a mass of tight curls under a tilted straw hat, with a bunch of artificial cherries bouncing on the brim.

'Just had my hair permed. Fairly roasted me, in this weather. And frightened the life out of me, too, when they wired my hair up to that electric machine! Do you like it?' Cissie chattered cheerfully. 'Doing anything next Friday? You're invited to my wedding reception. A kind of apology, on behalf of the Young family, for all that business with my brother,' she added confidentially.

'That's very kind of you, but ... ' Flora sought for an excuse. Cissie was never her friend, only a working acquaintance. And she desperately wanted distance between herself and Cissie's brother. 'My aunt ... '

'Oh, she's coming with Rab Lambie, and young Dr Anderson has promised to look in, too. Met your aunt in Byres Road this morning. Changed woman, isn't she?' Cissie marvelled.

'She's very involved with the new branches,' Flora murmured.

'Yes, she told me about it — and about you meeting my mother and Willie. I was really angry about that. My mother had begun to think that Willie wasn't so bad, but I've left her in no doubt. Since I've taken over, profits in the shop have just about doubled. She can't ignore what that means.' Cissie nodded knowingly.

'So Morgan and myself want our wedding to be a real celebration. Next Friday night, in the Partick Lesser Burgh Hall — Scotch broth, steak pie, peas and roast potatoes, and trifle. A real purvey, we're getting done!' Cissie finished with pride.

Flora found it difficult to stem the flow, for Cissie was buying a selection of their most-expensive cakes.

'They're for my wee party for the staff,' Cissie explained.

Flora tied together six fancy boxes and passed them over to the plump figure on the other side of the counter. She sighed with relief when Cissie almost danced happily out into the sunlight.

'Don't forget my wedding — Friday night! Bring a partner!' she called out.

'Is she the *bride*?' Margaret whispered incredulously.

Flora nodded. 'Yes, she's happily

besotted with her Morgan.'

She envied Cissie, so sublimely sure of being in love and loved in return.

★ ★ ★

At that moment, Mona was helping Nurse Laidlaw to lift Nadia from the bed to a cushion-filled armchair nearby. Nadia's head fell back weakly, although her eyes smiled warmly at the younger girl.

'Now for the war paint!' Mona exclaimed, cheerfully assembling creams and lotions on a small table. Keeping up a flow of light conversation, she applied the cosmetics to her stepmother's face with quick, deft movements.

It was satisfying after a few minutes to see the wan face become attractive once more. Then, with a quick flourish of comb and brush, she coaxed back some of the waves of Nadia's last set.

'Et voila!' Mona danced with the mirror in front of Nadia in mock pretence of a French coiffeuse.

Nadia's face lit up when she saw how attractive Mona had made her, and she smiled as, with a flourish, Mona displayed a pretty bedjacket. Then swiftly, with Nurse Laidlaw's help, she slipped it over Nadia's shoulders and tied the extravagant bows.

'Nurse Laidlaw, will you fetch my father from the study, and I'll get Loly to bring up the baby,' Mona said, ignoring the look of pique on the nurse's face. On no account was she taking the baby from Loly's care. Loly had saved his life, even Ralph Anderson had admitted that.

For the first five or six days they had watched helplessly as his grip on life became weaker. He couldn't feed properly. Eventually, Mona had gone down to the kitchen and wept, unable to bear listening to his cries.

Then Loly surprised them all by marching upstairs, going to the cradle and lifting the baby out. She put him against her bosom, and wrapped him and herself round in a large tartan shawl.

'The bairn's hands and feet are cold, and what's worse, his wee heart is getting no loving either, stuck in a cot. I was the eldest of ten in our family. Not the first sickly baby I've nursed,' she declaimed defiantly before carrying him downstairs.

Catriona McNeill left the house, returning within the hour with a young woman cradling a new-born baby.

★　★　★

Now, a week later, young Eric Alexander had changed from a whimpering weakling to a lusty infant, already fighting to dislodge the warm folds that cocooned him.

But it had not helped the atmosphere between Nurse Laidlaw and the housekeeper, now backed by Catriona McNeill. These two were sure of their superiority in rearing babies. Both of them had years of practical experience, and felt they had watched the baby being mishandled long enough.

Nadia was happily exhausted after half an hour of cradling Eric in her arms, and talking to her husband. She gave the baby back into Loly's care, still marvelling that this sleeping blond infant was actually her son.

'All I want is to be well enough to look after you and the baby,' she said wistfully.

'Given time, you'll get back your strength,' Stuart Alexander said in a guarded, yet gentle voice.

When Ralph arrived for his visit, Nadia was back in bed.

'Yes, young Master Alexander has been visiting, and slept all through his mother's cuddles!' Nadia remarked lightly, for she knew Ralph had insisted she must get out of bed after lunch and have the baby brought to her.

Ralph smiled and nodded, checking his patient's pulse. Already it was stronger. He'd thought it better that the infant was regularly prised away from the three in the kitchen, so that the bond with his mother was kept alive.

He foresaw the danger that Loly might look on the child as her exclusive responsibility, and perhaps even consider Nadia a hindrance.

Not that he was ungrateful to the little woman. Being the eldest of a large family, Mrs MacLaurin's experience of weak infants could not be bettered, and Catriona McNeill finding a nursing foster mother had been a live-saver for the baby.

When Ralph left the sick-room, Stuart Alexander beckoned him into the study. 'And how do you find my wife now?' he asked.

'She's getting stronger by the day,' Ralph answered.

'That's reassuring, because I must get back to Paris.'

At the surprised shock on the young doctor's face Stuart Alexander smiled a little bitterly. 'I must earn a living — all my assets are settled on my wife and daughter.'

'I think they believe you are home for good,' Ralph nodded towards Mona, who had just come into the room. 'Your father wants to go back to Paris now.'

'I was lucky enough to land a good position in Paris,' Stuart Alexander gently explained to his daughter. 'After all, I need money to live.'

'Will you come back? What about Nadia and the baby — your marriage?' Mona blurted out, shaken by this unexpected news. Her father had said little about how he earned his living in Paris.

'I can provide a home for them in Paris,' he said quietly. 'But I've hesitated to broach the subject with Nadia until she was stronger.

'You ... you must understand, Mona. I left because Nadia made it very clear she didn't want a failure for a husband. And my business was failing.' He looked at his daughter. 'I thought she would have explained that to you.'

'Your wife has spoken to me about that time,' Ralph interrupted quietly. 'She bitterly regrets her words. Remember, the pregnancy was, unknown to her, in its early stages. She was emotionally and physically drained.'

His words made Mona remember Nadia's irrational behaviour after her father left — ordering her out of the house, accusing her of conniving in his disappearance.

Mona had taken it for granted that having come home, he would stay. Suddenly, she saw how selfish that was. Working in Lambies', she knew settled employment was important. She needed to get back there herself — they wouldn't keep her position open for much longer. And she hadn't paid her father the courtesy of realising he was in the same position.

'Have you discussed any of this with Nadia?' she asked him.

'Now she's on the mend, I'll talk things over with her. But I need to get back — others are depending on me.' He sighed. 'Can I count on both of you to help me tell Nadia, so that the minimum of distress is caused? Nadia does tend to — er — dramatise.'

That afternoon the weather changed. It clouded over and there was a heavy downpour. Everyone in Lambies' welcomed the cooler weather, although Margaret Boulding grumbled

'That's it broken for the Glasgow Fair,' she complained. 'And I'm going down to Rothesay with the family.'

'That must be lovely,' Flora said wistfully. She'd never been away on holiday. Her mother disliked the idea, and there was never money to spare, anyway. She realised now there were many ordinary experiences she had missed when she lived with her parents.

Since lunch Flora had felt the tension in the shop heighten. Aunt Isa and Rab and Hugh Lambie were up in the office, interviewing Tom Miller from the wine counter. Already grocery's Andy Rees was smiling importantly. He had been given the manager's position in the Westergait shop in Partick.

When Dick and Harry, on the ham

counter, were told they would be called, they sent young Jamie Morton out to the gents' outfitters, two doors along, for new white collars. Then they took it in turns to slip off to the back shop and put the collars on and slick their hair back.

'I hear some of the Westergait staff are being brought in here to replace our people,' Margaret told Flora excitedly after a journey to the cool room. 'Three young men and a girl are in the back shop.'

When Flora went there a little later, she saw the newcomers by Mr Campbell's cubby hole. Revelling in his rôle, he was informing them of how things were done in Lambies'. The three young men seemed eager, but the young woman looked miserable.

Her hopelessness touched Flora.

All afternoon, one by one, the male assistants were called to the office, and most came out smiling broadly, happy with their promotion.

Tom Miller was to be in charge of the

ordering and distribution of the wine and spirit stock for all the branches, and he was to have one of the young Westergait men as an assistant.

Dick was to become the chargehand of the ham counter, and Harry was to go into the back shop to control stock.

Then, near closing time, came a big surprise, when old Mr Barclay came from the office to the kiosk looking for Flora.

'Miss Flora, please spare your assistant,' he said in his quaint, old-fashioned way. 'Miss Boulding's presence is requested in the office.'

Flora and Margaret exchanged mystified looks before Margaret hurried off. Ten minutes later as the doors were being closed she returned with Aunt Isa to the kiosk.

'Sorry, Flora, we're taking your new assistant for the grocery chargehand's job. She's the best person for it. And she'll have two of the Westergait men working under her.'

Aunt Isa paused, then added, 'Your

new assistant will be Miss Susan McMillan. She's back there. Her father used to own the Westergait shops.'

A few minutes later Flora was introduced to the sad-looking girl she'd seen earlier.

'I think you'll enjoy working in the kiosk,' she said kindly, trying to ease the girl's obvious misery.

'In the morning, my dear, come in a nice black dress or black skirt and white blouse and Flora will soon initiate you into the kiosk. You have to be a particularly refined person to work here — only quality goods are handled,' Aunt Isa said with brisk kindliness.

The girl nodded, avoided looking directly at any of them, and left.

'Poor lassie. She was kept at home and lived the life of a lady. Now her father is managing one of the shops he used to own, and her mother is going in as the second-in-command to keep an eye on him. Her whole comfortable world has crashed round her feet.' Aunt Isa shook her head. 'From the sale they'll probably manage to pay most of their bills, but their house will have to be sold for the rest.'

At closing time everyone normally rushed to do their last tidying and get out quickly, but tonight the shop buzzed with conversation as the staff huddled in little groups, discussing their new jobs.

Flora was pleased when her aunt came home on the tram with her. It had been so long since they'd spent any time in each other's company. Recently, Aunt Isa would arrive home very late, and rush off to the Byres Road branch first thing.

All the way home they talked non-stop, and it was only after they reached the first landing of their close that Aunt Isa stopped in mid-sentence.

'It's very quiet! Where are the children?'

Flora stood for a moment, aware of only the muffled music of Henry Hall's Dance Band from a distant wireless. The usual cries and laughter were absent, especially from the four young Macphersons and the three McDermids, who lived on opposite sides of the landing.

On a wet summer evening like this the boys would normally jump guiltily to hide their sixpenny ball, trying to pretend they hadn't been heading it to one another in the close.

The girls would be usually sitting on the stairs with their scrapbooks, swapping. Angels and cherubs were very popular, as were little girls with baskets of flowers, and crinolined ladies with poke bonnets.

They reached the next landing and old grey-haired Granny Wilson, all in black except for a cameo brooch at her throat, waited for them at her open door.

'Oh, Miss Rennie, first thing this morning the fever vans came — carted off every child in this close with scarlet fever!'

Isa and Flora were shocked, although the green ambulances were a familiar sight in Glasgow.

Infectious diseases like scarlet fever and the killer diphtheria were still the scourge of city children.

'Six weeks in hospital, and their hair cut off — a terrible trial for young children. Poor lambs!' Aunt Isa murmured sadly.

'The sanitary man came for the bedding to fumigate it, too. The blankets are like grey felt now,' Granny Wilson went on dolefully. 'Mind you, Mrs Macpherson's are always like that — but Mrs McDermid puts out such a lovely washing.'

'There's unemployment in the Macphersons' — I don't know how she manages.' Isa gently stopped the old woman, who loved a gossip.

Over tea, they discussed the illness in the close and Isa decided to inquire about the children later. And she talked about her own plans for being married quietly at the end of August.

Only immediate family were to be invited with perhaps one or two friends

— like Mona and Mrs McLaurin — and a few of the staff who had been with Lambies' for many years.

'And talking of weddings,' Aunt Isa exclaimed, 'Cissie Young's is on Friday night. Rab feels we must go, as the Youngs are an old Partick business. Will you ask Bartie to partner you?'

'No,' Flora said quietly. 'I can't!' She told her aunt that she'd refused Bartie's offer.

Aunt Isa was disappointed. Bartie was such a fine young man.

'Ralph Anderson's going, so you'll just have to ask him,' her aunt said decisively. 'You can't be on your own near Willie Young!'

She discussed Cissie's wedding with affectionate hilarity, unaware that her suggestion had alarmed Flora.

Two loud bursts on the door bell interrupted them.

'My, that's Mona!' Aunt Isa exclaimed, recognising the special ring.

Flora's spirits rose as Mona came in and threw her arms round her. 'I've aged! It's just over three weeks since I was here last, but it feels more like three years!' she cried. 'Tonight I'm sleeping next door. I just had to get away.' She explained about her father wanting to return to Paris.

'Ralph and I helped him break the news to Nadia.' Mona sighed. 'Ralph was marvellous, gently explaining, telling her she must get well and try Paris, even for a little, with young Eric.

'He painted a very romantic picture of the Left Bank, the artists on the steps of Montmartre with their easels, and famous writers frequenting the pavement cafés.' Mona laughed. 'Nadia actually stopped crying and listened, and started asking my father questions.'

Mona had realised that husband and wife needed to be alone to talk, so she made the excuse that she must go home, ready for her return to Lambies' the next day.

★ ★ ★

Later, Aunt Isa went downstairs to ask after the children, and Mona and Flora went over the landing to the opposite flat. It smelled musty from being closed up, and chilled, too. They lit the kitchen fire which Catriona McNeill had left set, and sat before it, hungrily catching up on each other's news.

Mona eagerly listened as Flora told her about the intrigues in Lambies', her new assistant and all the promotions.

Mona, in her turn, recounted how Mrs McLaurin had intervened with the baby. 'Quite amazing!' She laughed. 'Loly's hopeless in emergencies, but tiny babies are the exception.' She described the state of war between Nurse Laidlaw and the kitchen.

'I can't keep it a secret from you, Flora,' she suddenly exclaimed. 'Hamish and I are unofficially engaged. We hope to get married in October, but first he has to tell his mother!'

'I'm delighted!' Flora cried. When they first met she'd sensed Mona's deep hurt over the break with Hamish, brought about by his mother's meddling.

'I think she suspects things are serious,' Flora said, and told her of Mrs Buchanan's visit that morning.

'She won't be pleased!' Mona grimaced. 'You would have been her preference. She tried to steer Hamish in your direction.'

Flora nodded and smiled. 'But when we were out together, Hamish talked exclusively about you.'

Mona giggled. 'There was a time when I thought he preferred you, and I turned to Bartie, but he only had eyes for you.'

At this, Flora became serious, and confided in Mona about turning Bartie down.

Mona was surprised. 'I thought you were so well suited. Is there someone else?' she queried.

'Yes, I think there is,' Flora admitted, and explanations tumbled out.

How she'd rebuffed Ralph when he first suggested that they would make a fine couple. It had both surprised and shocked her, with his years of yearning after Kirsty. Then how unhappy she had been when Ralph then treated her like a stranger, and how, last time they'd met his quiet avowal of his regard had disturbed her.

Mona listened, wide-eyed. Flora was always so calm and in control of herself.

'What do you think?' Flora asked at last.

'Well, maybe his eyes were opened when that girl got engaged out of pique,' Mona reasoned. 'I wonder if he ever really loved her, Flora? Remember, he missed her parents' silver wedding to take you to the medical ball.'

'But he had to advance his career, so that he could ask Kirsty to marry him.' Flora rushed to defend Ralph's action.

Mona smiled shrewdly. 'When you really want to marry, you find ways. Hamish and I are going to live here. We only have to get a telephone installed. Between his junior partner's salary and my allowance we should manage — but first he has to tell his mother.'

For a few moments, both young women stared into the dancing flames of the fire, immersed in their own thoughts, the gentle patter of the rain on the window the only sound. Then the front door bell rang shrilly.

'Probably Aunt Isa back!' Mona said and hurried out to open the door.

Lots To Celebrate

Ralph! What a lovely surprise. Come in! Flora's here. What can we do for you?' When Mona led Ralph into the kitchen, she noticed for the first time that daylight was fading fast. She and Flora had been sitting by the dancing flames from the fire.

'Let's have some light!' She touched the switch. At once the bright electric bulb harshly lit the kitchen, and the cosiness of the firelight was destroyed. Mona immediately regretted it, because Flora, with no time to compose herself for this unexpected meeting, looked tense and vulnerable.

Mona pretended gaiety. 'Come and join us at the fire, Ralph!' she cried.

He nodded solemnly to Flora and took the chair Mona had placed between theirs. At once he explained he had come straight from the Central

Station, where he had seen Mona's father on to the night sleeper to London.

'He asked me to let you know immediately. He and Nadia agreed that the sooner he went, the quicker he'd return for his next visit.'

Mona was relieved to hear Stuart had arranged to come home every month until Nadia was fit to go to Paris with him. Now her wedding to Hamish could be arranged to coincide with a visit.

Ralph paused and looked appealingly at her.

'It would be of a great benefit to Nadia if Mrs McLaurin accompanied her to help care for the baby.

'Young Eric is doing so well in her charge, and he should be weaned on to baby foods in a few months.'

Mona sighed noisily. 'And you want me to persuade Loly to go to Paris?'

Ralph nodded. 'Your stepmother has no experience of young babies — and she is rather old to be starting.'

Mona looked thoughtful. 'Yes, I'll do it. It will suit my purposes very well if Loly is some distance from this flat!'

For the first time a smile softened Ralph's face. 'Are you and Hamish getting married?'

'How did you know?' Mona cried, and looked towards Flora — the only one who shared her secret.

'I'm not blind,' Ralph said quietly.

Mona laughed, realising it was merely a guess on his part. But she impressed on him that it must remain a secret until Hamish told his mother.

'Ah, yes, Mrs Buchanan! The formidable lady who tells everyone how they ought to order their lives,' Ralph said dryly.

'Even you?' Mona cried delightedly.

'Yes, she thinks my change of medical career in September is a foolish whim.'

'And why are you changing from family doctoring to train as a surgeon?' Mona asked him boldly.

'I've always had a hankering to be a surgeon,' Ralph said. 'But I had dreams of getting married, too, and general practice would have been more financially practical. Being a junior surgeon isn't very lucrative.'

'So you've shelved the idea of marriage for the time being?' Mona remarked wickedly, stealing a glance at Flora.

'The only girl I actually proposed to turned me down.' He glanced over at Flora, who was now blushing furiously.

She scrambled to her feet. 'You . . . you'll both have a lot to discuss about Nadia, and Paris. I'll see you tomorrow, Mona. Nice to see you again, Ralph.' She bobbed her head in both directions, and practically ran out of the room.

Back in Aunt Isa's flat, she went to her bedroom and stood, biting her lip.

Surely she herself was the only girl he had proposed to? Ralph always said he'd only ask Kirsty when he was in a proper position to do so — but she'd got engaged to someone else.

Flora was annoyed with herself. Why

had she bolted like that? Why could she not have brazened it out? Pretended that she was unaware of the implications of his words?

She sighed. She was such a coward — or was this just inexperience? She'd never had to cope with feelings like this. For a wild moment she wished she had agreed to Bartie's walking-out proposal. That would have settled things. After all, Bartie was amiable, easy going and he cared for her.

Then, just as quickly, her commonsense was in control. She didn't feel for Bartie as she did for Ralph, and she doubted if Bartie really cared deeply for her, either — at least, not as Hamish and Mona cared for each other.

She stood at the window, staring down into the street far below.

She was aware of her aunt coming in the front door.

'Met Ralph Anderson on my way up. He was delighted when I suggested you should be partners on Friday evening. He's got an evening surgery, but he'll see you there,' Aunt Isa announced.

'Oh . . . oh, yes, I forgot to mention it,' Flora said weakly. Although happiness swept through her at the thought that she'd see Ralph so soon.

★ ★ ★

In Lambies', next morning, there was a buoyant mood after the previous day's tensions. Mona's happy personality, missing for the last few weeks, helped, too. In their new positions behind the grocery counter with Margaret, were two of the Westergait men. She wore the white coat overall, denoting her new charge-hand status.

In the back shop, Harry, promoted from the ham counter, was instructing big Roddy McNeill, his new helper, on how he wanted the stock stacked.

Roddy was eager. He hated being a message boy, being so much taller than the others and wearing his dated knickerbocker suit, the daily butt of jibes from the other boys. But now he had been given a pair of brown dungarees and he was happy, especially about earning 15/- a week.

Eight o'clock passed that morning and Flora felt a spasm of annoyance. Susan McMillan, daughter of the ex-owner of the Westergait shops, had not arrived. Ten minutes later she appeared, white faced and red eyed.

'I'm sorry — I had a bad night and overslept!' she gasped when she came to the kiosk.

Flora wanted to retort that she, too, had had little sleep. But she remembered her own first day, and the terror she felt then. It must be doubly difficult for this girl, used to a life of leisure.

'You had your blouse and skirt ready.' Flora smiled. 'They look very nice — just what's required.'

She taught Susan how to wrap the fragile delicacies. Then as the morning wore on she realised she was treating Susan just as Aunt Isa had treated her, only allowing her to wrap while she herself served the customers. The truth was it was quicker that way.

Flora was a little on edge, too, wondering how the situation would be when Bartie came in. But she needn't have worried, for Bartie was still the same even-tempered person when she bumped into him in the back shop.

'It's all change here today,' he marvelled, watching as Harry and Roddy quickly stowed away his delivery. 'And you have a new assistant, too?'

'Yes.' Flora smiled, relieved that there was no tension between them, for she was fond of Bartie. 'Come and meet her. Maybe you can put a smile on her face — I think she's terrified.'

'So you're Susan!' Bartie shook Susan's hand warmly. 'Did you know I wanted Flora to walk out with me, but she refused? Maybe I'll just turn my attentions on you!' he teased her, and she gave a little giggle.

Flora was grateful to him as he stood flirting cheerfully for a few more minutes. When he moved off, there was even colour in Susan's face. Then Flora smiled, watching Margaret on Grocery waylaying Bartie before he went out — Bartie wasn't short of admirers.

At lunchtime Mrs McLaurin came in for some of Nadia's favourite cakes.

'She's not eating much yet, so I thought maybe a wee something fancy might tempt her,' the little woman explained.

Flora inquired about the baby, and the little housekeeper happily held forth on how well he was progressing.

'Of course, he's a real Alexander. Don't see a bit of the Brookes in him — that's her family!'

Mrs McLaurin lowered her voice. 'They were pawnbrokers. Plenty of money, but she keeps it quiet. She'd like people to think she was well connected.' She sniffed disdainfully.

Flora suppressed a smile. It was just as Mona said — the little housekeeper was a terrible snob. And it seemed her loyalty still lay with Mona's dead mother, who had come from a titled family.

From the glass partition of the office above the wines and spirits, Mona waved to Flora to delay Mrs McLaurin's departure. And in a minute Mona arrived at the kiosk wearing her outdoor clothes.

'Loly, I'm taking you out for lunch,' she declared. 'Now, don't argue — Catriona will see the baby is well looked after, and we'll only be an hour.'

'Oh, no! I'm not dressed!' Mrs McLaurin was horrified. Eating out called for genteel clothes.

'Rubbish! We're going to the Town Bakeries, not the Malmaison!' Mona winked at Flora as she linked arms with Mrs McLaurin and led her, still protesting, out of the shop.

Flora sent Susan for her lunch, and found it a relief to be without the strain of watching the girl fumbling with every task she was given. She wondered if this was how Aunt Isa had felt, watching her own first efforts.

* * *

An hour later Mona was back. She stopped at the kiosk, wiping imaginary sweat from her brow. 'That was hard work, but I finally convinced Loly it was her duty to go with Nadia to Paris. I said it was what my mother would have expected her to do!' She giggled.

'And the rentbook will be put into my name, for good measure. So Hamish and I will have a roof over our heads.' With that, she skipped off happily to the office, just as Aunt Isa came in.

'I'll take over while you have your lunch, Flora,' she said briskly, and was behind the counter before Flora had a chance to warn Susan of Aunt Isa's reputation. 'Young Dr Anderson's waiting outside in his car to take you. I said you'd go and fix up arrangements for Friday evening.'

Flora stood for a moment, feeling winded, then managed to nod before hurrying off to get her coat and hat.

Hugh Lambie was at the kiosk when Flora passed on her way to the door.

'Take your time. You don't have to hurry back!' He smiled.

'You look very nice — just right for lunch with an eligible young man,' Aunt Isa added.

Flora stopped in her tracks and glared at them, then glanced behind her at Mona, who was waving encouragingly from the office. And from the smiles and knowing nods from the rest of the staff, she felt there was a conspiracy.

But outwardly she was composed as she got into Ralph's car.

'I'm glad we'll be partners at the Young wedding. Willie is my least favourite person.' Flora was trying to sound calm. Then she noticed that the car was moving in the direction of the city. 'Where are you going? The Town Bakeries is just round the corner.'

'We're not going there. I've booked a table in the Crowther Arms, where we can do some serious talking to clear the air,' he said, staring at the road in front, as he negotiated the traffic at Eglinton Toll.

Gradually, Flora relaxed. It was silly for her to get into a state over Ralph. She had known him for so long, and being beside him like this seemed so right, so dearly familiar.

Soon he had parked the car and they were at the restaurant, being met by a waiter in white tie and tails. He showed them to a small table. Flora was surprised when the waiter bowed out, telling Ralph the lunch he'd ordered would be along in a moment.

Ralph smiled at Flora's perplexed face.

'I phoned earlier and chose all the things I know you enjoy.'

'Shouldn't you be out doing calls at this time of day?' Flora asked.

'Yes, but after I met your aunt in Byres Road this morning, I arranged with one of the partners to fill in for me. I told him how important it was.'

They were interrupted by waiters

coming in and serving their first course of hors d'oeuvres.

★　★　★

They ate in silence for a few minutes then the funny side of the situation struck Flora. 'Seems a very extravagant way of meeting to make arrangements for Cissie Young's wedding.'

'A perfect excuse to see you,' Ralph returned, smiling. 'Although this wedding will be totally unique,' he added wryly.

The soup, Cullen Skink, followed, a mixture of smoked haddock, potato, milk and cream, a dish her mother had made for special occasions.

'First time I tasted this was in your home,' Ralph reminisced. Flora was reminded that she hadn't had it since her mother died. But her attention was diverted by the waiter bringing in a silver ice bucket and stand, with a half bottle of white wine in it.

Ralph tasted the wine and nodded.

'Excellent. Nothing like a Chablis, properly chilled, to go with chicken cordon bleu! And we need wine for celebrating.'

'What are we celebrating?' Flora asked, as waiters carried in steaming silver salvers.

'My starting to court you properly. I made a real hash of it first time I tried,' Ralph said briskly.

'What do you mean?' Flora started, feeling a little nettled.

'Now! Now!' Ralph held up a restraining hand. 'I've spoken to your aunt, and she has given me full permission and encouragement.'

'You — you asked my aunt!' she exclaimed. 'But I'm not a child!'

'You act like one sometimes,' Ralph said bluntly. 'But then, so do I! Let's eat and I'll explain. It all started in earnest that night we went to the medical ball, and I thought Hamish was keen on you . . . '

Flora listened, hardly able to believe her ears. He'd told her then that Kirsty cared for him, but it seemed that, almost, simultaneously, he began to doubt if his feelings for Kirsty were as deep as he had always thought.

'Suddenly, I felt trapped. Almost overnight you had blossomed into an interesting and beautiful young woman who was in great demand. I didn't like it! I was especially frightened that you'd transfer that special closeness we'd always had and I'd taken for granted, to another man.'

Then he explained that when Kirsty got engaged out of pique, his doubts were confirmed.

Flora glanced up at him, and he grinned.

'Everyone was pleased when they met us together at the dinner, and some even told me they preferred you to Kirsty. Then, when I got the offer of a partnership and the old man thought you were my fiancée, I was so excited that I rushed in like a callow boy, and you rejected me.'

'What did you expect?' Flora said

flatly. 'For years you'd gone on about Kirsty and how wonderful she was.'

'So you made me suffer. I even tried to dislike you for a few days.'

'You treated me like a stranger!'

'But I couldn't keep it up. You were so gentle and dignified, no matter how awful I was. Then last night, quite out of the blue, I got some hope. Mona hinted that you were far from being completely indifferent. Are you?' He put his hand out and covered hers across the table.

'No, I'm not indifferent!' Flora said quietly, just as a waiter opened the cubicle door.

'Not now! Come back later!' Ralph snapped, his eyes still on Flora. 'Mona hinted you refused Bartie Darroch because of me. Did you?'

Flora was silent for a moment. 'Yes, I suppose I did.'

'Does that mean you'll marry me?'

'You'll have to ask me first!' Flora said impishly.

'Flora, will you marry me?'

'After some mature thought, yes, I think I will!'

'Yippee!' Ralph crowed like a school-boy, and at once the door opened and a waiter hovered in the doorway with another silver ice bucket, a bottle of champagne bobbing in the ice.

'Help me toast my new fiancée!' Ralph cried.

'Ralph, the expense!' Flora whispered as she took the glass he proffered.

'Hang it! I told them to bring it in when they thought the time was right. It's a unique occasion. I'll only get engaged once in my lifetime.'

It was after three in the afternoon when they finally emerged from lunch.

'Aunt Isa will think I've got lost!'

'She told me to take as long as we needed, and I don't want you to go back until my ring is on your finger. That's what we're going to do next.'

'Oh, Ralph, I could use my mother's engagement ring.'

'No! There'll be nothing secondhand about this engagement. And stop

315

worrying about the expense. I can certainly afford a ring — even if I won't manage many luxuries for you on a junior surgeon's salary.'

'You do realise I'll have to produce you at the family lunch on Sunday?' Flora teased.

'And there are my parents in Ayrshire for you to meet,' he retorted. 'But they'll love you!'

It was after five that evening when Flora finally arrived back at Lambies'. A cheer went up from the staff when she crossed the threshold, and it seemed every face, including the customers, was smiling broadly.

Hugh Lambie was at the ham counter. 'Let's see the ring!' he called.

'We all surmised that it was on, by the way the two of you were sitting outside in the car. And I couldn't be more pleased!' Aunt Isa smiled.

At closing time everyone crowded round to admire the diamond solitaire on her finger and wish Flora well. At last only Susan McMillan and Margaret

Boulding were left.

Susan sighed. 'You're lucky. You'll be leaving this place. I hate it!'

'You were lucky to get the kiosk!' Margaret snapped. 'You might have got my old job, brushing out the back shop every morning and spreading fresh sawdust.'

'Yes, but I'm not very competent. The only good thing today was meeting that big carrier,' Susan said innocently.

Flora saw the bleak look return to Margaret's face. Bartie was always pleasant to her, but never flirted lightheartedly as he had with Susan this morning. Poor Margaret.

★   ★   ★

On Friday evening, after the late closing, Flora caught a tram and travelled in the evening sunshine to the West End of the city. She was to meet Aunt Isa and Rab Lambie at Cissie's reception.

Flora felt nervous as she went in,

317

unaware of how attractive she looked in a blue floral dress with a large white collar, and matching revers, and cuffs on the three-quarter-length sleeves. The little white hat, gauntlet gloves and shoes gave her a cool elegance.

'Flora Lochart! I heard you looked like a film star now.' Mrs Letham who used to share the early shift at Young's newsagent's, suddenly barred Flora's way. 'Cissie invited far too many folk, so you've got to queue to get fed. And Willie Young stormed out because she won't have drink even for a toast, her being so into temperance. Were you ever engaged to him?' she ended abruptly.

'This week I got engaged for the first time, and that was to Dr Anderson,' Flora answered quietly.

Mrs Letham's round face lit up. 'I knew there was something — so you were the doctor's intended all along!'

She turned and called to several other friends who knew Flora from her Partick days. They crowded round, eager to see her engagement ring and give her their sincere good wishes. They directed her to where Aunt Isa and Rab were waiting.

Aunt Isa looked annoyed. 'Willie Young's old mother's just been here. She took great pleasure in telling me Willie's getting engaged tonight to a classmate of yours, Agnes Keir. But my news of your engagement wiped the smug look off her face. Thought she was scoring a point off us!'

Flora shuddered at the thought of Agnes being engaged to Willie. Poor girl — out of the frying pan into the fire, for Agnes was a drudge to her ne'er-do-well father and brothers.

Flora caught sight of Agnes standing beside Mrs Young, looking happily pleased with herself. Her bleached blonde hair was waved close to her head, with rigid curls spaced out on her forehead, an almost exact replica of Jean Harlow's latest style.

But then, Agnes was a film-star fanatic. Maybe it was a good thing she escaped from life by going to the pictures several times a week. It would help when she was married, too . . .

'I think after Ralph comes, we should all leave,' Rab suggested, surveying the crowded room. The long table down one side of the hall was crammed with people eating, and others were standing waiting for a place.

Space was being made now for the dancing to begin, to jaunty tunes from a little three-piece band.

The bride, her veil askew, her white dress already crumpled, was heading a long line of couples, ready to start off with her new husband, the old Scottish country dance, Strip the Willow.

When Ralph arrived and heard the news, he insisted that he and Flora wait and dance an old-fashioned waltz together.

As they reached Mrs Young, he stopped and exchanged a few pleasantries. Then, on behalf of himself and his fiancée, he smoothly congratulated Willie, who had just reappeared, and wished Agnes well on their engagement.

Flora found when they continued waltzing that she was trembling, and Ralph tightened his grip on her waist.

'Willie is an episode in your life that's finished,' he whispered. 'This dance will impress on everyone's mind that you're *my* fiancée!' And he steered her round the floor, accepting the good wishes showered on them from the other dancers and onlookers, many of them his patients.

★   ★   ★

Back in the Shawlands flat, Aunt Isa and Flora made tea and sandwiches. They all ate hungrily as they had not had a meal at the wedding.

Later, Rab drained his third cup of tea and set it down on his saucer. 'And now what plans have you young people made about where to live after you are married?' he asked.

'We'll have to rent a small flat for the first few years,' Ralph said.

'Isa and I were discussing that. We think that the pair of you should take over this flat, furniture and all. We're starting fresh, with nothing from either of our homes going into our new place.'

Flora looked at Ralph, delight on her face.

'That's a marvellous wedding present,' Ralph said gratefully.

'Just perfect!' Flora breathed. It had been a problem, for Ralph didn't want to use the money from her father's books.

And Mona and Hamish being their next-door neighbours made everything doubly perfect. But she kept quiet, as her friend's engagement was still unofficial.

She almost laughed aloud as the door bell gave Mona's double ring, and in moments she and Hamish were in the room. Mona's eyes were red from weeping, and she looked embarrassed when she saw Rab and Ralph were there.

'Sorry, I forgot about the wedding.

We . . . I . . . just needed some advice from Aunt Isa,' Mona murmured.

'Come on, lassie, we'll help put right whatever has made you cry,' Rab Lambie said gruffly, pushing forward a chair.

It was Hamish who spoke.

'Mona and I intend getting married in the autumn — quietly, because of my father's precarious health. We let my mother know our plans tonight, and she immediately refused to come to the wedding. But, as far as I'm concerned, it goes ahead no matter what!' he finished grimly.

'We so wanted her to be pleased.' Mona sighed, and wiped away tears.

'Seems Mrs Buchanan hopes she'll put a damper on the proceedings, so that you'll postpone the wedding or even cancel it!' Aunt Isa said briskly. 'She wants to be in control.'

'These two want to set their date within the next few months.' Rab Lambie nodded to Ralph and Flora.

'Why not get together and have a

double wedding? You two girls are the best of friends. And — with Isa's permission — we'll offer you our house in the West End for the festivities.'

'Yes, that great big parlour with the billiard room off it! Just made for a wedding. And two brides coming down that staircase!' Aunt Isa cried, her eyes sparkling with tears of happiness at the thought.

Flora and Mona looked at one another, open mouthed, as the offer with all its implications sank in.

'Oh, it would be wonderful, both of us getting married together!' Mona breathed in wonder.

Then she shrieked with delight as she heard about Flora and Ralph's tenancy of Isa's flat after their marriage.

Hamish relaxed and smiled with relief at the happiness on Mona's face as she and Flora hugged.

Meeting Flora was the best thing that ever happened to Mona, and that she'd be next door when they married was the best news he'd heard today.

He knew his mother's unconcealed dislike had wounded Mona deeply. She'd come between them once before, but now he was determined that she wouldn't interfere. And if he knew his mother, she'd be at the wedding.

'It all sounds like a fairytale.' Flora smiled a little tremulously, unable to voice her deep gratitude to Aunt Isa and Rab Lambie.

She understood why Aunt Isa was marrying him.

Her heart was full — especially when she thought back to the beginning of the year, and how bereft she had been. When it seemed all she cared for had come to an end. But now, standing with Ralph's arm about her and her friends around her, she knew she was going to be blissfully happy — especially when Ralph whispered in her ear.

'We'll make it a wonderful life — together!'

DANGER COMES CALLING

Karen Abbott

Elaine Driscoe and her sister Kate expect their walking holiday along Offa's Dyke Path to be a peaceful pursuit — until a chance encounter with a mysterious stranger casts a shadow of fear over everything. Their steps are constantly crossed by three men — Niall, Steve and Phil. But which of them can they trust? And what is the ultimate danger that awaits them in Prestatyn?

NO SUBSTITUTE FOR LOVE

Dina McCall

Although recently made redundant, nurse Holly Fraser decides to spend some of her savings on a Christmas coach tour in Scotland. When the tour reaches the Callender Hotel, several people mistake Holly for a Mrs MacEwan. Furthermore, Ian MacEwan arrives to take her to the Hall, convinced that she is his wife, Carol! Although Ian despises Carol for having deserted him and their two small children, two-year-old Lucy needs her mother. Holly stays to help the child, but finds herself in an impossible situation.

LOVE'S SWEET SECRETS

Bridget Thorn

When her parents die, Melanie comes home to run their guest house and to try to win the Jubilee Prize for her father's garden. But her sister, Angela, wants her to sell the property, and her boyfriend, Michael, wants a partnership and marriage. Just before the Spring opening, Paul Hunt arrives and helps Melanie when the garden is attacked by vandals. After the news is splashed over the national papers, guests cancel. Then real danger threatens. But who is the enemy?

OUT OF THE SHADOWS

Judy Chard

Why does Carol Marsh, the new receptionist at the country inn in Devon, have to report to the police regularly? Why does she never ask for time off and rejects all attempts by the owner, Norman Willis, to be friendly? Then, Norman's wife is found dead in suspicious circumstances. Could Carol have had some part in her death? Yvonne's relationship with her husband had deteriorated since Carol's arrival. Maybe Carol and Norman have a deeper, more sinister relationship than that of employer and employee.

THRILLINGLY GOOD BOOKS
FROM CRIMINALLY
GOOD WRITERS

CRIME FILES BRINGS YOU THE LATEST RELEASES FROM
TOP CRIME AND THRILLER AUTHORS.

SIGN UP ONLINE FOR OUR MONTHLY NEWSLETTER AND BE THE FIRST
TO KNOW ABOUT OUR COMPETITIONS, NEW BOOKS AND MORE.

VISIT OUR WEBSITE: WWW.CRIMEFILES.CO.UK
LIKE US ON FACEBOOK: FACEBOOK.COM/CRIMEFILES
FOLLOW US ON TWITTER: @CRIMEFILESBOOKS

'FLAWLESS' JAMES PATTERSON

They made him a target.

He will make them pay ...

STOP AT NOTHING

MICHAEL LEDWIDGE

THEY MADE HIM A TARGET. HE'LL MAKE THEM PAY.

When a private jet crashes into the Caribbean sea, diving instructor Michael Gannon is the only person on the scene. Finding six dead men and a suitcase full of cash and diamonds, Gannon assumes he's the beneficiary of a drug deal gone wrong.

However, it seems one of the passengers was the Director of the FBI – despite the official story that he died of natural causes in Italy. Suddenly pursued by a shadowy cabal of the world's most powerful and dangerous men, Gannon will only survive if he unravels a terrifying conspiracy.

But those determined to kill him will learn that Gannon's past holds its own deadly secrets . . . and the hunters soon become the prey.

Available to buy

HEADLINE